ROBOUTE GUILLIMAN

LORD OF ULTRAMAR

THE HORUS HERESY®

More Ultramarines from Black Library

THE FIRST HERETIC
Aaron Dembski-Bowden

KNOW NO FEAR
Dan Abnett

MARK OF CALTH
Various Authors

BETRAYER
Aaron Dembski-Bowden

THE UNREMEMBERED EMPIRE
Dan Abnett

PHAROS
Guy Haley

THE HONOURED
Rob Sanders

MACRAGGE'S HONOUR
Dan Abnett & Neil Roberts

Audio dramas

HONOUR TO THE DEAD
Gav Thorpe

CENSURE
Nick Kyme

RED-MARKED
Nick Kyme

STRATAGEM
Nick Kyme

THE HORUS HERESY®
PRIMARCHS

DAVID ANNANDALE

ROBOUTE GUILLIMAN
LORD OF ULTRAMAR

BLACK LIBRARY

For Margaux, for when we stand, and for when we catch each other.

A BLACK LIBRARY PUBLICATION

First published in 2016.
This edition published in Great Britain in 2016 by
Black Library,
Games Workshop Ltd.,
Willow Road,
Nottingham, NG7 2WS, UK.

10 9 8 7 6 5 4 3 2 1

Produced by Games Workshop in Nottingham.
Cover illustration by Alex Boyd.

A CIP record for this book is available from the British Library.

ISBN 13: 978 1 78496 441 2

See Black Library on the internet at

blacklibrary.com

Find out more about Games Workshop
and the world of Warhammer 40,000 at

games-workshop.com

Printed and bound in China

THE HORUS HERESY®
It is a time of legend.

Mighty heroes battle for the right to rule the galaxy. The vast armies of the Emperor of Mankind conquer the stars in a Great Crusade – the myriad alien races are to be smashed by his elite warriors and wiped from the face of history.

The dawn of a new age of supremacy for humanity beckons. Gleaming citadels of marble and gold celebrate the many victories of the Emperor, as system after system is brought back under his control. Triumphs are raised on a million worlds to record the epic deeds of his most powerful champions.

First and foremost amongst these are the primarchs, superhuman beings who have led the Space Marine Legions in campaign after campaign. They are unstoppable and magnificent, the pinnacle of the Emperor's genetic experimentation, while the Space Marines themselves are the mightiest human warriors the galaxy has ever known, each capable of besting a hundred normal men or more in combat.

Many are the tales told of these legendary beings. From the halls of the Imperial Palace on Terra to the outermost reaches of Ultima Segmentum, their deeds are known to be shaping the very future of the galaxy. But can such souls remain free of doubt and corruption forever? Or will the temptation of greater power prove too much for even the most loyal sons of the Emperor?

The seeds of heresy have already been sown, and the start of the greatest war in the history of mankind is but a few years away...

Volcanic ash leads to fertile soil, but it also leads to a theoretical misapprehension. Emphasis on the positive outcome can result in the memory's blindness to the original destruction. If the source of the ash is not taken into consideration, ash may settle over a dead land. The error in the theoretical results in the misapplication of the practical. Exemplum: Consul Gallan's betrayal. In its wake, despite the death of Consul Konor, Macragge is unified. This is because I understood Konor's error, and my own. We underestimated the consequences of frustrating Gallan's ambition. My elevation occurred in a context where ambition was not itself devoted to the service of a greater unifying cause. Gallan had no true cause. He had only the need to preserve the power of a decayed aristocracy. My Father gives the Imperium a cause and thus its unbreakable strength. This principle, once applied to all social, cultural, and military formations, ensures a cohesion that surpasses the vagaries of individual ambition.

– Guilliman, *On Loyalty,* 45.22.xiv

ONE

THOAS • RECLAMATION • SYMBOLISM

One empire came to Thoas to crush another.

The empire of order and light arrived in the form of an armada. If the eyes of the other empire had turned to the void, perhaps they would have witnessed the final approach. They would have seen a swarm of blades. Each blade was a ship thousands of yards long. The greatest of them spanned fifteen miles from stem to stern. It was both sword and mountain chain. From the surface of Thoas, it would have appeared as an elongated star, moving with unalterable purpose with its smaller brothers. A constellation of war filling the night sky.

But in the second empire, there were no eyes to look upwards, or none to understand what they saw. This was not an empire worthy of the name. Yet it had held a dozen systems. One by one, they had been ripped from its grasping claws. Now the empire unworthy of the name was reduced to its core. Its seat of strength. Its source of contagion.

It did not see its doom arrive. If it saw, it did not understand. If it understood, it did not care. Such was its nature. That reason alone was enough to warrant its extermination.

* * *

Remark 73.44.liv: The visibility of the leader at significant moments of a campaign carries its own signification. It reinforces his interest not just in the goal, but in those sworn to carry it out. The leader who lacks these interests invites and deserves defeat.

Roboute Guilliman stood at the lectern of the bridge of the *Macragge's Honour*. Below him, in a tiered space the size of an arena, the level of activity had risen in urgency, but proceeded with no loss of calm. Officers performed their tasks with the same efficiency as the servitors. The bridge hummed with the sound of human machinery, gears meshing smoothly, readying for war.

Guilliman had been at his station five hours already, ever since the translation to the system. He was here to witness and to be witnessed, as was proper. *Addendum to 73.44.liv*, he thought. *Interest cannot be feigned.* He would insert the correction to the manuscript later.

He had watched Thoas grow large in the forward bridge windows. He had seen its details resolve themselves as the layers of augur scans built up the composite picture of the target. The forward elements of the fleet were now at low anchor, awaiting his command for the next stage of reconnaissance.

'Another message from Captain Sirras,' said Marius Gage.

'Reconfirming that his Scouts are ready?' Guilliman said.

The Chapter Master Primus of the XIII Legion grinned. 'That would be correct.'

'He's contacting you directly now?'

'We were together on Septus Twelve in the Osiris Cluster.'

'In the hive?'

'Yes,' said Gage. 'We both made it to the surface in time to see the flares of the fleet burning when the Psybrid ships sprung the ambush.'

'So he presumes this gives him leave to bypass the chain of command?' Guilliman asked.

'The Twenty-second is still without a Chapter Master,' Gage reminded him.

'I haven't forgotten.' The orks of the Thoas Empire had taken Machon's head in the final stages of the campaign to purge them from the Aletho system. 'There will be a new Chapter Master before we land on Thoas. The current lack does not justify Sirras trying to make an improvisational end run around my timing decisions.'

'An official reprimand?' Gage asked.

'No. But inform him that if he contacts you again, the next voice he hears will be mine.'

The old warrior nodded. His features were worn by his centuries of campaigning, and had been weathered into wry, intelligent cragginess. He walked a few steps away to vox the captain of the 223rd Company.

'Wait,' Guilliman said. *Remark 73.42.xv: It is the duty of the soldier to accept an order without a rationale being provided, but the absence of a rationale should never be the default condition.* 'Let him know the scans are still being collated. He isn't waiting on a whim. He's waiting for a worthwhile target.'

In the bridge window, another layer of topographical detail was added. The image of Thoas sharpened. Coastlines changed from fractal abstractions to specific geological characterisations. The world was becoming a real place. It was tidally locked by its blue star. Half of the planet burned forever while the other half froze. The Ultramarines fleet was anchored over the region of the terminator, where twilight and dawn would never end.

Guilliman examined the sphere. He frowned. 'Magnification of the northern tropic,' he said.

The image grew.

'Increase magnification.'

There.

A cordillera ran along a north-to-south-west diagonal down the western region of the largest continental mass. To the east, the land was wrinkled with mountains, canyons and plateaus for close to five hundred miles. To the west was a vast plain that reached almost to the coast before it ran up against a narrower, lower chain of peaks. In the western flank of the cordillera, Guilliman saw lines that were too regular. There were structures there, almost as big as the mountains in which they nestled.

'Biomass readings in this sector?' Guilliman asked.

'A very high concentration of orks, lord,' the Augur Master reported.

Given the inviting geography of the plain and the easier slopes of the foothills, that was to be expected. 'Compared to the other principal land masses?'

'Higher,' the officer confirmed.

'Are you seeing this?' Guilliman said to Gage.

'I am. Are those human?'

'Records about Thoas are fragmentary in the extreme. To date I have found only two references to any form of human colonisation.'

'Those are big,' said Gage. 'This was more than a colony.'

Guilliman nodded. 'It was a civilisation.' The prospect was pleasing. If there had been human colonies in the other systems reclaimed from the orks, all traces had long since vanished. That such signs would appear on this world, where the final battle against the greenskin empire would take place, was a gift of inestimable value. *If* the ruins were human. 'Tell Sirras we have a target for him.'

'Evido Banzor has Scouts ready for a low orbit drop too,' Gage said. 'Part of the 166th, under Captain Iasus.'

'Good. Send them both down. I want their eyes on the ork dispositions with particular respect to those structures. The Thoas campaign begins there.'

'"*When presented with a choice of beginnings, choose the one with meaning,*"' Gage quoted.

'Remark 45.xxx,' said Guilliman. 'Flatterer.'

'Merely a manifest truth,' Gage said, his eyes on the traces of immense ruins.

'Our captain honours us with his presence,' said Meton. His voice was a whisper, inaudible except over the vox. The orks were a long way beyond earshot. The visible ones, at least. Meton was observing proper discipline, taking no chances as the squads made their way up towards the ridge.

'Theoretical – our captain is merely eager to get his hands dirty with greenskin gore,' Sergeant Phocion said.

'Practical – your captain would like you both to shut up,' said Eleon Iasus. They were both partly correct. There was no compelling necessity for him to have left the *Praetorian Trust* to accompany the Scouts on their reconnaissance. There was no dereliction of duty either, though. As a sergeant, he had held Phocion's position for decades. And he had cleared his venture with Chapter Master Banzor. Yes, he wanted the feel of Thoas' surface under his boots as soon as possible. There was more, though. *Theoretical: there is no such thing as superfluous advance knowledge of the battlefield. Practical: where possible, add first-hand experience to intelligence gathered from a distance.* He wanted to see the ruins. He wanted to know what would be the epicentre of the campaign.

The Scouts of the 166th prowled along the western spines of the cordillera to the south of the ruins. They maintained vox contact with the squads from the 223rd coming in from the north. Both had come down by Thunderhawk, deposited on ledges a short way down the east-facing slopes. There had been no contact with the enemy. There was nothing to attract the orks here. The mountainsides were sheer, the valleys narrow and barren. There was nothing to fight over, and no room to fight either. The tectonic upheavals in this region had been so violent, so sudden, and involved so much compression that the chains of the cordillera were as narrow and sharp as rows of fangs.

Footing was treacherous. Iasus and the Scouts climbed, working their way up the nearly vertical mountain face. The sharp folds of the granite caught and held shadows. Both of Thoas' moons were full, but the mountains had draped themselves in a dark more profound than night. Even with his enhanced sight and the night-vision lenses, Iasus was blind when his climb took him deep into the vertical crevasses. He climbed by feel, reaching up, digging his gauntleted fingers into the cracks, holding onto jagged protrusions with certainty they would not crumble beneath his weight. Long before he reached the top, the drop below, a fall from dark into dark, would have been far enough to kill him.

He was glad he had come. Each foot of the climb instilled a greater sense of Thoas in him. The theoretical knowledge transforming into the practical experience.

The ridge was as sharp and narrow as he had imagined it would be. He stood on the edge of an immense, rocky sawblade. It was difficult to stand.

'Theoretical,' said Meton. 'If we drive the orks into these mountains, we'll smash them.'

'We'll smash them regardless,' Iasus said. The Scout was correct, though – an army that retreated into the mountains would be devoured by their teeth. And if by some chance the orks survived, if they went any further east, they would reach sunrise, and be cremated.

Iasus looked down. The orks were all to the west, the clans gathered in their hundreds of thousands on the plain near the base of the foothills and on the gradual slopes of the start of the mountains.

And they infested the ruins.

Phocion's squad had advanced to a point several thousand yards from the nearest structure. The edges of the ork horde were directly below. The growls and snarls of the brutes rose to the heights like the roar of a violent surf. There were orks on the plain too, but the bulk of their numbers were sticking to the high ground. There was no reason to think these greenskins were intelligent enough to understand what force was coming for them, but they were readying for battle. As the Ultramarines had taken apart their empire, they had left no survivors in their wake. The beasts lacked anything but the most rudimentary technology. They had nothing resembling interplanetary vox communication. Yet somehow, they knew. Some collective instinct of the species told the greenskins to prepare.

Iasus turned his attention from the orks to the ruins. He raised magnoculars to his helm lenses. The structures snapped into clearer focus. They were badly damaged. The upper levels had collapsed. Apertures gaped, open to the winds and storms of Thoas. The roofs were gone from the buildings he could see. They were still colossal. They were constructed of huge blocks carved from the mountains. Iasus estimated that each brick was larger than a Thunderhawk. He saw pillars as high as Warhound Titans. They too were monoliths.

So much had fallen that the original shape of the ruins was difficult to discern. What Iasus could make out looked like terraced pyramids, each the size of a small city. The terraces were narrow in proportion to the levels' soaring height. The effect was less of broad, squat structures, more of towering massiveness. The architecture was aggressive and brutal even in its decay. But it was not alien. Colossal as the scale was, the shape of the vaulted apertures was recognisable. There were smaller doorways in the walls, openings where orks had to bend down to pass through.

'The greenskins did a thorough job,' Phocion said.

'So will we.' Iasus lowered the magnoculars. 'This was a human world once. It will be again.'

Guilliman met with his Chapter Masters in his compartment. Twelve Chapters had come to rout the orks from Thoas. Eleven Masters stood in a precise arc before Guilliman's desk. With them were two captains – Hierax, the senior captain of the leaderless 22nd, and Iasus, who had earned his place at the audience with the knowledge he had brought back from Thoas.

That, Guilliman knew, was what was widely assumed to be the reason for the honour granted to Iasus. For the time being, he did nothing to correct that perception.

Behind the primarch, the crystalflex walls showed the orb of Thoas below the *Macragge's Honour*. The flagship was at low anchor, in geosynchronous orbit above the great plain at the foot of the cordillera. The ruins were not visible at this altitude. Even so, if Guilliman turned around, his gaze would zero in on their location in the mountains.

He gestured to the data-slates on his desk. 'The reports from the Scouts are conclusive,' he said. 'Humans once called Thoas home. They built great cities. That civilisation has fallen, but humans will lay claim to this world once more, and towers will rise again. There is more. Thermographic imaging and geologic auguries have revealed the presence of an extensive network of caves beneath the ruins.'

'Do we know how deep they run?' Atreus, Chapter Master of the Sixth, asked.

'No,' said Guilliman. 'There are significant radiation blooms in the area too. They made imaging difficult. We know the tunnels are there. Beyond that, we're indulging in conjecture. An unhelpful application of the theoretical.'

He stopped speaking. He observed the two captains. Their

stances were perfectly formal, perfectly motionless. The Chapter Masters were more relaxed in their bearing. They understood that this compartment was a space for inquiry and debate, and the free exchange of views. Here was where theoreticals were worked over and modified, demolished and reconfigured. Absolute deference to his authority here was counterproductive. It undermined what he hoped to accomplish.

Though Iasus and Hierax might as well have been statues, Guilliman could still detect minor variations in their bearings. Iasus was content to wait until he was called upon. His stance was one of simple patience. Hierax, on the other hand, was on the verge of an explosion. He was leaning forwards slightly. Awareness of rank and the nature of his position held his tongue. The reason for his presence urged him to speak.

Guilliman relieved him of the dilemma. 'You have a recommendation, Captain Hierax?' he said. *Surprise me*, he thought. *Say something other than what I'm expecting.*

'The ork infestation on Thoas is the worst we've seen in this campaign.'

'This *is* the heart of their empire,' Guilliman pointed out.

'Exactly,' said Hierax. 'We should rip it out at a stroke. There are no humans in those ruins. There haven't been for a long time. There is no reason to hold back.'

'No holding back,' Guilliman echoed, keeping his tone neutral.

'The Second Destroyers will purge the orks from Thoas within the day.'

'Along with all other life.'

'Primarch–' Hierax began.

'Captain,' Guilliman interrupted him, 'how expedient were you planning to make this invasion? I assume you imagined keeping Thoas intact, so that eliminates cyclonic torpedoes. Virus bombs, then? Would you go that far?'

Hierax said nothing at first. His face was closed, so carefully neutral it lacked any expression at all. Like Gage, Hierax joined the XIII Legion on Terra. His rough features bore layers of scars. His face had a geologic history, as if roughened by successive lava flows. The nobility of the Ultramarines shone in his armour. Hierax himself embodied the harshness of war. The Destroyers were the necessary violence of the Ultramarines. They represented the moments when the heart was hardened, and the terrible act undertaken. They lived their name. They were the blood spilled by the blades of the Great Crusade. The Destroyers were not its hope, its promise and its creation. When Hierax spoke again, his voice was strong but cold. He already knew that Guilliman would refuse his recommendation.

Just as I know what it will be, Guilliman thought. *I'm disappointed. It would have been nice to be proven wrong.*

Hierax took a breath. 'If necessary, yes,' he said. 'Our mission...' He stopped, realising he had overstepped. The mission was not his to define.

'Go on,' Guilliman urged. 'Speak freely, captain. If we cannot do that in this space, half of its utility vanishes.'

Hierax nodded his thanks. 'Theoretical – our mission here is one of extermination. Practical – the most efficient way of ending the enemy while minimising our expenditure of lives is though the weaponry of the First and Second Destroyer companies.'

'You see no other value to the world?'

'Mining will still be possible after the worst of the radiation subsides. Its agricultural possibilities are poor. What Thoas offers will survive the worst we can do on the surface.'

'I see.'

The Chapter Masters remained silent. *You know me well,* Guilliman thought. They knew the debate was about more than a tactical decision.

'Captain Iasus,' Guilliman said. 'You were on the surface. What are your views?'

'I respectfully disagree with my brother's evaluation.' The captain of the 166th was younger than Hierax, and a native of Macragge. His features were far less worn than Hierax's. The long, livid scar that ran from his right temple down the length of his jaw made his profile seem even more aquiline. 'The value of Thoas is more than industrial. There was an important culture there. Its memory should be preserved.'

'That culture failed,' said Hierax.

'It did,' Guilliman agreed. 'Does that mean it should be expunged from our collective memory? Do we have nothing to learn from it? Does that mean its stand against the orks does not deserve to be commemorated? That there were no battles worthy of song?'

'It does not,' Hierax admitted.

'No, it doesn't.' Guilliman placed his hand on a stack of bound vellum manuscripts on the side of his desk. 'There is no tactical value to the remembrancers on our vessels. They contribute nothing to the battlefields of the Great Crusade. What they contribute in between the battlefields is inestimable. The records of the pacifications. The celebrations of victories. The memorialisation of the fallen. The analyses of the recovered cultures. This is the living tissue of the Imperium's culture, Hierax. Even the dead civilisations are part of the human story. They have a life beyond the dust of their citizens.'

He turned to look at Thoas. Most of the planet was a dark brown, but it was far from dead. Its atmosphere was turbulent with the flashing energy of storms. The coasts were green with vegetation. Thoas was alive. Even with the cancer of the orks upon it, it was alive. He would not kill it. And he would not kill its history.

'The orks took Thoas from humanity,' he said. 'We will take it back. We will not lose its heritage in the process.'

'The radiation levels…' Hierax began.

Guilliman raised a hand. 'I know,' he said. 'They are high in the region of the ruins. Will we make them higher yet? We come to reclaim and to build. We will take Thoas back, and we will build a new civilisation here. Of course it will surpass what was there before, but it will also honour this world's history.'

He smiled at Hierax. 'Do you understand, captain?'

'I do.' The Destroyer's tone was flat.

I wonder if you do, Guilliman thought, even more disappointed. Hierax was a good officer, but he was limited. He also symbolised a larger problem Guilliman had seen growing in the Legion, one the time had come to deal with.

'The Nemesis Chapter stands ready to deploy when and as ordered,' Hierax said.

'I'm sure the Twenty-second does.' Guilliman's use of the numeral designation sounded like a rebuke. 'And deploy it will.'

'All of it?' Hierax asked.

Guilliman raised an eyebrow at the shade of anger in the question. More evidence of the necessity of what he was about to do. He was glad he had asked Hierax to be here. Listening to the captain had confirmed him in his resolution.

'No,' he said. 'Not all of it. There are some actions that will not be necessary.'

Hierax's lips thinned.

'The time and the place must be the correct ones,' Guilliman said. 'These ones are not.'

Hierax bowed his head. He said nothing.

To the Chapter Masters, Guilliman said, 'You have seen the intelligence gathered by the Scouts of the 166th and 223rd Companies.' He emphasised the credit. He had just informed Hierax he would, once again, not be seeing action. He wished the captain to know, also, that the contribution of his Chapter had value.

'We land in the plain?' Banzor asked.

Guilliman nodded. 'Your thoughts?'

'A good staging area. The orks have the high ground, but our presence will draw them down.'

'Their high ground is a dead end,' said Atreus. 'If we force them back there, that is where they die.'

'And they will be a diminished enemy in retreat,' Klord Empion of the Ninth mused.

'That practical depends on the theoretical of the orks abandoning the ruins,' Banzor said.

'When have greenskins ever resisted the bait of a fight?' said Gage.

'Good point,' Banzor admitted.

'We see no chance the ruins are so important to them that they might hold their ground?' said Vared of the 11th.

'Highly unlikely,' Guilliman said. 'It would be unprecedented.'

'"*The unprecedented*,"' said Iasus, quoting *Axioms* 17.vi, '"*is the catalyst for adaptability. Do not hope to expect every eventuality. Meet it instead.*"'

Hierax frowned at the other captain's temerity. Gage raised an eyebrow, amused.

'The very words,' Guilliman said, grinning.

He ended the briefing a few minutes later. The target was clear. So was the strategy. This wasn't an attack that called for finesse. It would have bored Lion El'Jonson or Fulgrim senseless. Angron might have appreciated the straightforward application of overwhelming force, though he would have been baffled by the decision to capture and preserve the ruins. This was the strategy the enemy and the goal called for, though, so it was the strategy that would be employed. *The difference between doctrine and dogma is the gulf between triumph and defeat.*

'Evido,' Guilliman called to Banzor as the Chapter Masters and the captains filed out of the compartment. 'A brief word, if you would.'

Banzor walked back to the front of the desk. Gage remained where he was, off to the side and between the desk and the crystalflex walls. Guilliman had told him some of what he had planned, but not all. He was visibly startled by the fact Guilliman had asked the Chapter Master of the 16th to stay. Banzor merely looked puzzled.

When the doors had closed behind the others, Guilliman said, 'What is your evaluation of Captain Iasus?'

'In what sense?'

'In general. And in his ability to command, in specific.'

'A fine warrior. An excellent captain.'

'He inspires loyalty?'

'He does. He doesn't just lead from the front. He's fought at one point or another with just about every squad in the company. They know he knows what they do and what they need to do it.'

'So his mission with the squads was typical rather than unusual.'

'Exactly.'

'Adaptable, then.'

'Very.'

'And his overall command of the company? I appreciate his fine knowledge of the workings of the squad, but a captain needs to be more than a very flexible sergeant.'

'You need have no reservations on that score, primarch. The 166th has been exemplary under his leadership.'

'I'm glad to hear it. Thank you, Evido.'

Banzor left, still puzzled. He had questions, but he did not ask them. Guilliman did not offer him answers. He had not made a final decision yet. Until he did, there were no answers for Banzor's questions.

Guilliman moved to his seat behind the desk. He looked at Gage. The Chapter Master Primus looked less puzzled. *He's guessed*, Guilliman thought. Even so, he would not open this particular discussion with Marius. He wanted the quiet of his own counsel first.

Gage understood. Gage knew him well. So Gage spoke of something else. 'Thoas,' he said. 'Are the ruins that important?'

'You think I should let Hierax off his leash.'

Gage shrugged. 'The Destroyers haven't been planetside at all on this campaign.'

'Their tactics and their weapons have not been called for. We are not fighting that kind of war.'

Gage hesitated. 'Will we ever?'

'For those companies as they are presently constituted, I hope not.'

'"As they are presently constituted"?' Gage asked.

Guilliman waved off the question. 'Later,' he said. 'To answer your first question – yes. The ruins are that important.'

'Why?'

'Their symbolism. Thoas is a culmination. We will crush the ork empire here. We will reclaim a world that we *know* was once a human one. Another piece of what is and must be inherent to the Imperium will be restored.'

'All that would be true regardless of the state of the planet.'

Guilliman gave the old veteran a sideways look. 'Since when are you such an advocate for the Destroyers' way of war?'

'I just don't think we should reject Hierax's approach out of hand.'

'I haven't. I said the symbolism of the ruins is important. It is for two reasons. We are not destroyers, Marius. That isn't why my Father created us. It can't be. It won't be. So preserving a city, even a dead one, is important. Especially now.'

'Because of the one we destroyed,' Gage said after a moment.

'Yes,' said Guilliman. 'Because of the one we destroyed.'

Monarchia. Lorgar's pride. The city raised to glorify the

Emperor. The city razed because it had deified the Emperor. A place of architectural wonder. A beautiful city. The XIII Legion had come to the jewel of Khur. The Ultramarines had taken possession of the city. They had rounded up the population. They had reduced the empty city to ash and glass.

The people of Monarchia had committed no crime. They were loyal to the Emperor. *Loyal to a fault*, Guilliman thought. They were guilty only of believing the lie taught them by Lorgar, a lie Lorgar had believed himself. The memory of the grief on Lorgar's face during his confrontation with the Emperor haunted Guilliman. It had been the terrible agony of a son punished for doing what he had thought would be pleasing to his father.

The Ultramarines had destroyed a city and the spirit of its populace to chastise Lorgar. To humble his pride.

To make a point.

Symbolism.

'I keep wondering,' Gage said, 'why us?'

'Because my Father could trust us to perform the task as it needed to be done. Would you have wished it on any of the others?'

Gage shook his head.

'And Angron might have enjoyed himself,' Guilliman added. 'We did what we had to. We were deliberate. We were dispassionate. My Father's chastisement was measured.'

With a sigh, Gage said, 'I did not feel measured when we flattened Monarchia.'

'None of us did.' The destruction had taken its toll on the Word Bearers. That had been its purpose. There had been a cost for the XIII Legion too. 'We suffered a blow because of what we did there. We took that blow because it was necessary and because we could stand it. Do you see what Thoas can be for us?' *Symbolism.* He tapped a data-slate, summoning the picts Iasus and the Scouts of the 166th had captured. 'There is majesty there. Majesty worth preserving, and worth building upon. We will take back this city, and in time we will see a new civilisation rise here.'

'We'll be creators again,' Gage said.

'Thoas will wash the bitterness of Monarchia from our mouths.'

As he spoke, Guilliman turned his seat to look out through the crystalflex at the planet below. He saw the plain where his legions would land. His eyes locked onto the spot where he knew the ruins stood. He thought of absent cities. He tried to make himself think of cities yet to be, not of cities unmade. He failed. He thought of both.

He thought of the force of symbolism, and of the choice he knew he had already made.

Though there are circumstances where elevation may be inevitable, it must never be perceived as such. The alternative is disastrous: the foregone conclusion bypasses the necessity of the theoretical. What is preordained can never be questioned. Thus, ossified tradition rules without the benefit of reason. In the worst cases, the errors it leads to are so far from identified and corrected that reality itself is misread, misrepresented and denied. Elevation must therefore always have a clear reason. Its justice must be undeniable. Inevitability must only be perceived in retrospect.

No principle is beyond the perception of envy. Consul Gallan demonstrated this. His ambition led him to see my elevation as manifesting the wrong sort of inevitability. He could only see with the eyes of a member of the old order on Macragge. His misunderstanding was thus itself inevitable. This perception is the spawning ground of schism and betrayal. Key, then, is the creation of a military culture where such perception is unthinkable. Such a culture goes beyond its warriors being able to see that elevation is based on merit. Rather, they take this fact as an unquestioned truth, as self-evident as the truth of the Imperium itself.

– Guilliman,
Essay on the Principles of Command, 8.17.xxiii

TWO

ELEVATION • TRADITION • THEORETICALS

'At least we were warned,' Sirras said. 'At least we know why we're here.'

Hierax grunted. Sirras was right, but the mercy was a slight one. The shock was still real. The humiliation was just as sharp. He was spared being caught off-guard during the ceremony. But he had had several hours for the injury to fester. His anger had developed layers. And teeth.

The warriors of the XIII Legion's 22nd Chapter stood to attention, row upon row, in the vast landing bay of the strike cruiser *Cavascor*. They were here to await the arrival of their new Chapter Master.

The ten captains of the Nemesis Chapter formed an honour line before the bay doors. Hierax, the longest serving, was at the centre. Sirras stood to his right. The captain of the 223rd was a veteran of almost as many battles, but he looked decades younger. His skin was tight around his skull, and his short hair was so pale it was almost translucent. On Hierax's left was Laches, captain of the First Destroyer Company, who had succeeded Phalaris when he had been elevated to Chapter Master.

'Why is he doing this?' Sirras asked. His aquiline features were pinched in anger.

'Because it is his will,' Hierax said. He did not want to talk about the elevation. The other captains were silent. He had not spoken with any of them since the announcement had reached the *Cavascor*. The humiliation was too deep a wound. He did not trust his reactions. His anger might break out, and he was determined to salvage his honour at least.

Klaxons sounded. The bay doors were about to open.

'Our new Chapter Master is here,' Hierax said. It took him a moment to realise he had spoken aloud.

'It should be you,' said Laches.

I thought it was going to be, Hierax thought. This time he held his tongue. He disliked displays of hurt pride. He would not let his become a spectacle.

'It should be you,' Sirras echoed.

The bay doors rumbled open. The void shield held the atmosphere in as the Thunderhawk *Masali Spear* entered the bay. Its retro exhaust nozzles blasted downwards as its main engines cut out. The gunship lowered itself to the deck on a cushion of flame. The rumble of its arrival still echoed as its forward assault ramp lowered.

Hierax braced himself for the ceremony. He gave in to his pride then. His face was still, and he was silent. His thoughts were a roar. *It should be me.* He had held the thought away for hours. It had been at the root of his pain, yet he had forbidden himself to articulate it. It was too strong, though.

It should have been me. I am proud. I am angry. But I am not wrong.

Heavy footsteps from within the Thunderhawk. They would be those of Marius Gage, Hierax thought. The Chapter Master Primus come to do the honours. Under protest? Hierax wondered. He hoped so. *Gage knows damn well what an insult this is.*

Not just to me, but to the entire company. Gage was Terran, after all. He understood. He had to.

It was not Gage who first emerged from within the Thunderhawk's troop hold. It was Guilliman. Gage appeared a few steps behind him. They stopped at the base of the ramp.

A ripple passed through the psyche of the company. Sirras gasped. Hierax's resentment became confused. He was no less angry. He had been furious since the briefing aboard the *Macragge's Honour*. But to keep his anger directed at Guilliman... That was impossible. Not when he stood there, his presence filling the bay.

Hierax was confused. The primarch's actions enraged him. Yet he could not look upon the primarch with fury.

He is the greatest of us. All that we are comes from him.

And this too was true. Hierax's memory of his first sight of Guilliman had the strength and vividness that came only with revelation, with epiphany. Hierax had been fighting in the XIII Legion for decades when the Emperor found his lost son. Decades of victories, decades of glory, but decades too of an absence, perpetually felt if never understood. And then the day had come when Guilliman stood before the Legion, and the absence had vanished. Hierax had experienced a completion that was individual and collective. He had gazed upon his leader and his father, and known himself to be an Ultramarine. Guilliman towered over them all. His face was carved by war, his eyes sharpened by study. He was a living idol fashioned into something that partook of the human while being greater than that state.

Hierax relived that moment every time he saw the primarch. He had known that awe and gladness the day before on the *Macragge's Honour*. He knew them again now. So he did not know what to do with his anger.

But it did not leave him.

'Legionaries of the Twenty-second Chapter,' Guilliman said. 'You have suffered loss, and you have fought on.'

Oh, that was true. Though not all of the 22nd had been permitted to fight as they knew how. For most of the campaign, the Destroyers had remained on the ship. Guilliman had given Chapter Master Phalaris leave to send them against dug-in orks on the barren moon of Agrigentum V. *Where we couldn't do any harm*, Hierax thought. The company as a whole had seen little action, relegated to reserve status. The bitter irony was that Phalaris had not been killed in the field. One of the ork vessels, its construction so crude Hierax wondered if the brutes even understood they were traversing the void, had slammed into the superstructure of the *Cavascor*. The ork construct, more stone than metal, had disintegrated. The bridge of the strike cruiser had been gutted. It still had not been fully repaired. Command was spread across multiple secondary control centres across the ship. The casualties had been severe. Along with most of the mortal bridge officers, four captains had died. So had Phalaris.

As senior captain, Hierax had overseen the elevation of new captains. The interim command of the company had fallen to him. Phalaris had been senior captain himself before becoming Chapter Master. That mechanism for the passing of the mantle was a tradition in the 22nd. It had served the Chapter well. The 22nd cohered. Its warriors had a sense of their Chapter's distinct identity, and that point of pride helped sustain them during the frustration of inaction.

Now the tradition was being broken. Violently.

'The strength of the Thirteenth Legion,' said Guilliman, 'is the strength of each warrior, and the strength of every warrior. Our sum is a greater whole, one that depends on every individual, yet transcends all of us, without exception.' He paused, then repeated, 'Without exception.'

Gage's left eye twitched. A tiny gesture, and a fleeting one. Hierax saw it. The Chapter Master Primus was startled.

But you know as well as we do who the Chapter Master is. So why are you surprised? What other meaning did you hear?

'I have taught you my precepts,' Guilliman continued. 'They continue to evolve, as they should. War is fluid. We must be too. The theoretical is worthless if it becomes a certainty. It *must* be tested. The practical is worthless if it is a ritual, unsupported by anything except the habit of use.'

That was pointed, Hierax thought. The primarch was teaching the Chapter right now. *So why does this feel like a chastisement? Haven't there been enough of those of late?*

'Our Legion is adaptable. It must always be so. This is the truth that undergirds the theoretical and the practical. We must embody what we believe, or those beliefs mean nothing. Empty cant will surely result in defeat, and it deserves no less.'

Guilliman paused again. He swept his gaze over the assembled Chapter. Hierax felt the touch of those eyes. *He sees us all*. It should not be possible. Not so many thousands in a few seconds. Yet Hierax had no doubt. *He sees us and he knows us.*

But if he knows us, came the question, came the doubt, *why is he doing this?*

He just told you, Hierax answered himself. *This is why he has been speaking. He wants us to understand.*

I don't though. I can't.

'Legionaries of the Twenty-second,' Guilliman said. 'You have a new Chapter Master.'

More bootsteps now from within the gunship.

Guilliman turned as the warrior appeared. 'Chapter Master Eleon Iasus, I welcome you to your new command.'

Iasus' armour was resplendent. Newly polished, its hue reflected the lighting in the bay with the blue of indomitable purity. Hierax stared at the new marking on his right pauldron:

a winged skull, and the XXII of the Chapter numeral. The iconography drove home the truth of the new state of things even more forcefully than Guilliman's greeting. The die was cast.

As one, every legionary saluted Iasus. He crashed his fist against his breastplate in return.

Several long seconds of motionless silence passed. The necessary gestures had been accomplished. Hierax looked at the tableau formed by Iasus standing just forward of the assault ramp, flanked by the primarch and the Chapter Master Primus. Iasus faced his captains. The ranks of the battle-brothers completed the frame.

Behold the Twenty-second, Hierax thought. *The last moment of what we were has passed. The first moment of what we will become is about to begin. I wonder if I will recognise that form.*

'You look as unhappy as Hierax,' Guilliman said.

Gage had been watching the *Cavascor* recede as *Masali Spear* set course for the *Macragge's Honour*. He turned away from the viewing block. Guilliman was looking at him with patient amusement.

Gage did not share in the humour. 'I'm worried, not unhappy,' he said. 'Hierax most definitely is unhappy, though, and he's not alone.'

'I know he is, and I didn't expect him to be.' Guilliman's eyes narrowed almost imperceptibly, but their focus became las-precise. They bored though Gage's soul. 'I know you don't expect me to change my mind.'

'Of course not.'

'But…'

Gage hesitated. He had been debating with himself whether to bring the subject up or not. He had not *known* Guilliman had chosen Iasus as Chapter Master until embarking for the *Cavascor*. He had guessed, but Guilliman had made it clear his own counsel was enough on this matter. It had not been Gage's place to intrude. Now he was inviting Gage's thoughts. *Too late to make a difference*, he thought. *So to what purpose?*

Greater understanding, he decided. The primarch always wanted to know more. His hunger for information was insatiable. Always more data, before and after actions, always collating, always refining. Very well, then. Gage would tell him what he thought. There would be consequences attendant on the elevation of Iasus. If they could not be stopped, they should at least be discussed.

'Have you considered the impact on the Chapter of passing over Hierax for Iasus?'

'What would make you think I haven't?' When Gage didn't answer at first, Guilliman said, 'The fact that I made that decision at all?'

Gage thought through his response. 'The Twenty-second's character is… non-standard.'

'To put it mildly.'

'I don't mean the composition of the units.' Though that was certainly part of its individuality. The 22nd was a patchwork of specialised companies. Destroyer squads were rare in the other Chapters. Nemesis had two full companies. 'I mean in its sense of identity and its traditions.'

'So did I. Go on, though, Marius. I'm listening.'

'The proportion of Terrans is high compared to most of the Chapters. It is less than it was, but its influence is strong.'

'So it is.'

'The Terrans are a minority there now too, I believe, but they make up most of the officers.'

'And even those originally from Ultramar have adopted their culture, rather than the other way around.'

'Yes.' Gage wondered why Guilliman was encouraging him to say what the primarch already knew. He guessed that somehow he, not Guilliman, was the one who was meant to be acquiring new information, or new understanding, from the dialogue.

'And?' said Guilliman.

'The successor to a fallen Chapter Master has, until today, been the senior captain.'

'So it has.'

'A mechanism not unusual in the other Chapters,' Gage added.

'Very true. You anticipate particular consequences.'

'I do. Theoretical – this break with established practice will be perceived as a deliberate targeting of the Twenty-second.'

'Precisely because the practice is so common elsewhere.'

'Yes.'

'Go on,' Guilliman said.

'Iasus is not even a member of the Twenty-second, never mind senior captain. Theoretical – his elevation will be perceived as an insult at best. Theoretical – unhappiness with the mere fact of his command could lead to consequences on the battlefield.'

Guilliman stirred. 'Clarify that, Chapter Master Primus.'

'Reduced efficiency. Second-guessing up and down the chain of command.' He had not meant more than that. Anything worse was truly unthinkable, and beyond the wildest theoretical.

Guilliman nodded. 'I won't dispute your reasoning. Those are possibilities.'

'Then why…?'

'Because all of your analysis is correct. The Twenty-second *is* distinct. It *is* more Terran in its character than the other Chapters. It *does* have traditions of its own that have governed its internal functioning.'

Gage was baffled. 'Its effectiveness on the field has never been in doubt.'

'No, it hasn't. Yet.'

'I still don't understand.'

'The culture of the Twenty-second has a strong Terran

influence, and that influence is itself shaped by the Destroyer companies.' Guilliman had never made a secret of his distaste for Destroyer tactics. Even so, he had never disbanded them.

'We haven't purged the Destroyers from the Legion tacticae.'

'And I won't. At the same time, I see a necessity to reduce their influence. *Nemesis*,' he said, and grimaced. 'We are not the Twelfth Legion, Marius. To have an entire Chapter adopting that name should give us pause. The Great Crusade is a force of enlightenment, liberation and reclamation. I honour my Father with creation, not destruction.' He gestured at the viewing block next to him, filled with the reflected light of Thoas. 'The extermination of the orks is a means, not an end. *Nemesis*. That is not a term of creation.'

'Will you forbid the use of the name?'

Guilliman shook his head. 'That won't be necessary.'

Gage began to see the strategy behind the elevation of Iasus. 'Theoretical – short-term disruptions caused by the breaking of traditions may lead to longer-term stability after the period of readjustment.'

Guilliman began to smile. 'Agreed.'

'Practical – appoint an outsider as leader. The necessary adaptation will result in the desired change in culture.'

'Yes,' said Guilliman. 'The point isn't to alienate the Twenty-second. The point is to integrate it more fully into the wider culture of the Legion. The process is not a painless one.'

No, Gage thought. *It certainly isn't.* He opened his mouth to speak again, then thought better of it.

Guilliman noticed. 'You still aren't convinced.'

He wasn't. The short term concerned him. He was worried about how prolonged that short term might be. He was worried about the immediate effect on the battlefield, and the longer-term consequences that might flow from that. Disturbing theoreticals spun out from the recent practical.

'What it comes down to, Marius, is I trust Captain Hierax and his brothers, perhaps more than they do themselves.'

'I see,' Gage said, remaining noncommittal. Then he changed his mind. 'That is precisely what I'm worried about,' he said. 'If they lack trust in themselves, what then?'

Guilliman frowned. He looked at Gage as if he were speaking gibberish. 'There is a difference,' he said at last, 'between the theoretical and the nonsensical speculation.'

Mobilisation was only hours away. The armada had moved into its final disposition. The ships were ready to begin the drops. The orks could measure their reign over Thoas in hours. Hierax could feel the rising energy reaching across the void from vessel to vessel. The culmination of this war was approaching. He knew it. And he would be watching it from orbit.

He pushed the thought back down. There were too many shards of anger rattling around in his head. He had to keep them contained. He was about to speak with his new Chapter Master.

Phalaris' quarters had remained empty after his death. Hierax was grateful for that. Despite the internal assumption across the 22nd that he would succeed Phalaris, propriety and tradition had dictated he not occupy those chambers until his elevation. He had been spared the humiliation of removing himself from the quarters. There was one shard of anger with which he did not have to contend.

He was the first of the captains to meet with Iasus. The Chapter Master was respecting seniority. Hierax had half-expected he would meet with the Macragge-born Lobon first. When this did not occur, Hierax was furious at his own pettiness. Lobon, meanwhile, was at least as angry as Sirras over the elevation of Iasus.

Hierax stopped outside the iron doors to the Chapter Master's chambers. He knocked. The doors slid aside into the stone of the corridor wall. The study beyond was a space that was darker and heavier than Guilliman's compartment on the *Macragge's Honour*. The round crystalflex window on the void took up less than half of the far wall. The lumen strips along the walls where they met the high ceiling were subdued, giving the impression that the only light came from the orb above the desk.

Iasus stood behind the desk. He smiled when Hierax entered. 'Thank you for coming, captain,' he said.

Hierax gave him a brisk nod. 'The honour is mine,' he replied. He didn't expect Iasus to believe that any more than he did. He did not, though, let his bitterness infect his tone. There would be no insubordination in anything he said, or in how he said it.

Iasus' smile became pained. 'No,' he said, 'I really do think the honour is mine.' He gestured to the iron-and-wood seat before him. 'Will you sit, captain? I think we have a lot to discuss.'

Hierax nodded again, and accepted the invitation. Iasus sat also. They faced each other across the desk. Hierax had encountered Iasus a few times before, on the battlefield. The meetings had been brief. Hierax had placed no importance on them then. He knew Iasus by reputation. Word had spread about the captain who had made a point of fighting alongside every squad. Hierax could see the potential strategic value of the policy. Deeper knowledge of the squad level could translate into more effective deployment of the company as a whole. Today, though, he was not inclined to view Iasus' methods in the most favourable light. *If you think you'll be able to curry favour that way in the Twenty-second Chapter*, he thought, *you'll find we're less impressed by such methods*.

Iasus said, 'You expected to be where I am sitting.'

'I expect nothing except to serve.' Hierax spoke with his jaw clenched tight.

Iasus' eyes turned cold. 'I do not accept that answer,' he said.

Hierax glared at him. The Chapter Master was several decades younger than he was. How many more campaigns had Hierax fought in? Dozens, at least. Iasus had not experienced the cataclysm of Osiris. He had not seen the destruction of a quarter of the fleet in a single battle. *Your experience is shallow next to mine*, he thought. *How dare you think you can command me?*

He can because he is Chapter Master, he reminded himself.

He mastered his temper. 'I should rephrase,' he said. 'I knew there was no certainty of my elevation. There was the expectation born of tradition.'

'So I understand. And you should understand that finding myself here was not what I expected. I did not seek this office, Captain Hierax. I had no ambitions to leave my company and my Chapter and take the place I daresay was seen as *destined* for you.'

'I didn't think you had,' Hierax said. That was the truth. He resented Iasus' presence, but he did not envy him his task.

'Good. Then at least we have the beginnings of common ground on that point.'

Optimist, Hierax thought.

'I am fully aware of the situation we find ourselves in. The appointment of a Chapter Master who has not served with the Chapter is unusual enough.'

'Unique, I believe,' said Hierax.

'And the nature of the Twenty-second makes the event doubly so.'

'Agreed.'

'I think we can also agree the primarch doesn't act on whims.'

'We can,' Hierax said. His words sounded odd in his head. He wasn't sure if he believed them. Whether he did or not, either possibility was disturbing. If he admitted the truth of what Iasus said, then he needed to think carefully about the deeper implications of what Guilliman had chosen to do with the Nemesis Chapter. The impact of the appointment would go far beyond questions of hurt pride and the tension created by the arrival of an outsider. Iasus shared none of the traditions of the 22nd. If he even knew of them, he would have no reason to follow them. He might well feel compelled not to. His command would be a wind of change through the Chapter. If Guilliman had thought through the consequences, then Iasus, whether he knew it or not, was here to dismantle the Chapter as it existed now, and had for its entire history.

If Guilliman did not foresee what might come...

Hierax shut down that line of reasoning. It was absurd. It was dangerous. He believed it was possible for the primarch to be mistaken. He did not believe Guilliman could be blind.

'I think we understand each other so far,' Iasus said. 'Let me clarify things a bit further. I am under no illusions about my command. I know it is not welcome. But I also know I was placed here for a reason, and *you* must know that I intend to carry out my duty. I respect the achievements of the Twenty-second, and I respect all its warriors. I would be respected in turn. But if I am not, I *will* have my authority respected, because of the place from which it derives.'

'Of course,' Hierax said.

'We are agreed, then?'

'About what?'

'About what must be done. I accept the nature of the Chapter's feelings towards me, but I will have discipline. It will be enforced, and its enforcement begins with the captains. With you, senior captain.'

Hierax kept silent and still until he mastered his temper. 'I am as conscious of my duty as you are of yours,' he said at last. 'I have given you no reason to see me as derelict.'

'You are insulted.'

Hierax met and held Iasus' gaze. He said nothing.

Iasus said, 'I have no wish to injure your pride further.'

The corner of Hierax's left eye twitched slightly. The implied critique of his priorities stung. His temple throbbed with anger.

'But,' Iasus continued, 'I believe it necessary to be abundantly – even excessively – clear at this juncture. The Twenty-second has a storied history. It lost a great leader in Phalaris. I will do everything in my power to ensure a continuity of glory. To that end, I will need your help, Captain Hierax.'

'Your orders will be followed. Without question.' The words shouldn't need to be spoken at all. What did Iasus think? That the 22nd's legionaries were capable of insubordination?

Not overtly, he found himself thinking. *But subtly? Unconsciously, perhaps? How many different ways might there be to undermine an unpopular officer?*

Iasus nodded, apparently satisfied. 'I believe you,' he said. 'Implicitly. I think, too, that we will have to speak again. Often. In greater depth.'

'I am at your disposal, Chapter Master.' He could think of few things he would enjoy less.

'Thank you, Captain Hierax.'

Hierax chose to take the words as the cue the meeting was over. He stood to go. Iasus looked as if he was about to say something more. He thought better of it, and nodded to Hierax.

Hierax strode from the chamber, his shoulders stiff with contained anger. The doors closed behind him with a metallic scrape and bang. His effort to hold in his rage narrowed his vision. He did not see Sirras walking down the hall towards him. He was startled when the other captain stopped beside him.

'Well?' Sirras asked. 'What should I expect?'

Hierax forced his attention back to the present, away from past humiliations and future injuries. 'Exactly what you think,' he said.

Sirras grimaced. 'He means to remake us in his image, then.'

'He will say it is the primarch's image, no doubt.'

A snort. 'He presumes a lot.'

'Does he?'

'What do you mean?'

'His elevation can't be the result of a whim.'

'No.'

'Then the remaking is the primarch's will.'

Sirras stared past Hierax, his face thoughtful, his brow dark. 'A change of some kind clearly is,' he admitted. 'But not whole-sale, surely.' He blinked, then looked at Hierax. 'Do you think that's what Iasus plans?'

'Not consciously. I don't think he'll even realise all the ways he'll be changing our culture. He won't know that the traditions he's ignoring even exist.'

'If he doesn't know about them,' Sirras said, more softly now, 'there will be no reason for him to destroy them.'

'What do you mean, if he doesn't know about them?'

'Our traditions are worth preserving, brother. Lobon agrees with me.'

Our traditions. Lobon of Macragge and Sirras of Terra speaking with one voice. They belonged to the Nemesis Chapter together. Their birth-worlds were irrelevant. Wasn't this exactly what Guilliman wanted from the Ultramarines? Didn't he seek precisely a loyalty to the corps that transcended the attachment to an individual world? *We are what we should be*, Hierax thought. *Why would you change this?*

He agreed with Sirras. Of course he did. The traditions should be preserved. Even so, the vehemence of Sirras' tone coupled with how quietly he was speaking made Hierax uneasy. 'What are you suggesting?' he asked.

Sirras frowned, puzzled by Hierax's caution. Then his eyes widened. 'What did you think?' He sounded alarmed now. His voice was louder.

'I really don't know.'

'I will follow our Chapter Master's orders implicitly.'

'As will I.'

'But I will resist the destruction of who we are.'

'How?'

'We will find ways,' Sirras said. 'We'll know the struggle when we encounter it.'

'Resisting change may mean resisting Iasus. If it comes to that...'

'We won't let it.'

Hierax didn't trust Sirras' confidence. It was blind. There was no way Sirras could anticipate the nature of those struggles. 'Iasus may push hard.'

'We'll convince him not to.'

'Oh?'

'One way or another.' He held up a hand in anticipation of Hierax's objection. 'I said I would never disobey his orders. You know I never would.'

'Yes,' Hierax said. 'I know that.' So what was Sirras planning? Was he thinking of undermining Iasus somehow? Working to make his command untenable so that Guilliman felt compelled to relieve him? Hierax was torn. There was no common ground between him and Iasus. That was already obvious. Yet when he tried to imagine *one way or another* of pushing back against the Chapter Master, he recoiled. 'We have to find a way,' he said, 'of convincing the primarch of the value of what we represent.'

'A positive intervention, you think.' Sirras did not sound convinced.

Hierax sighed. His shoulders were stiff from the iron of his anger. He felt no warmth for the legionary on the other side of the iron doors. He hated even the distant hint of insubordination even more. 'Do you think he isn't suspicious of how we will respond to his leadership?' he asked.

'He's no idiot. I know that much from his reputation.'

'Exactly.' He turned to go. 'He's expecting you.'

Sirras didn't move. 'Where are we, then?'

'We are captains of the Twenty-second, and we will prove what that means.'

Hierax walked away before Sirras spoke again.

'A culture is a living thing,' Guilliman told Gage.

They were aboard the *Macragge's Honour* once more. Gage had said nothing on the rest of the journey back. Guilliman decided to draw him out again. There was something else Gage needed to understand. The Chapter Master Primus' concerns over continuity and tradition made this an opportune moment.

They were walking towards the bridge. The final preparations for the assault would begin in less than an hour. Guilliman turned off before they reached the main approach to the bridge, heading for his compartment once more.

'A culture,' he said, 'is created by its constituent citizens. In turn, it shapes them. It has a reality that transcends the collection of individuals.'

'Yes,' said Gage.

'"Yes"? That's it? Am I boring you, Marius?'

'You are about to make a point,' Gage said. 'I'm letting you make it.'

The primarch grunted. 'You are not subtle, Chapter Master Primus.'

'I never claimed to be.'

'Quite. So, we grant the transcendence of a culture.' He held up a finger. 'A *viable* culture.'

'Yes.'

Guilliman felt the corner of his mouth twitch upwards. 'The viable culture, then, takes on an importance that itself is superior to any one individual.'

'Ah,' Gage said, sounding disturbed.

'Do you see where I'm heading?'

'I think I might.'

They reached Guilliman's compartment. He led the way inside. 'I have documents for you to read,' he said.

'Why?'

Guilliman stopped at his desk. He turned around slowly. 'Because I wish you to,' he said.

Gage brought himself up short. He saluted. 'I misspoke,' he said. 'I did not mean…'

Guilliman waved away the apology. He turned to the desk. He picked up one of the data-slates and took it to Gage. Before passing it to the legionary, he said, 'Do you understand what I have been saying?'

'I think I do.'

'The Imperium is such a culture. That intent lies at the heart of everything my Father has done.'

Gage nodded, emphatically. On this point, he needed no convincing.

'What he has done for the Imperium is what I have – what I *am* – attempting to do for the Thirteenth Legion.'

'You *have* done it,' Gage said.

'I haven't finished,' said Guilliman. 'The work is still in progress. The Twenty-second Chapter, for example.'

'But you aren't insisting on the uniformity of all Chapters.'

'No, I'm not. Total uniformity is not a characteristic of a culture. That is a feature of the machine. But consistency is something I demand. Consistency and coherence. The unexpected in war can be disastrous. Theoretical – prepare for the destruction of an entire Chapter or worse. Practical – ensure any other Chapter can take the place of the fallen one. There *must* be a continuity of expertise and tactics across the Legion.'

'Agreed,' said Gage.

'Theoretical – the cultural integrity of the Legion must and will surpass the presence of *any* constituent element. *Any*.' He gave the data-slate to Gage. 'This is the practical.'

Gage took the slate. He scanned the titles of the documents on the screen.

'This is a work in progress,' Guilliman said. 'I will continue to refine it. The essential principles, though, are there. You will, in due course, and in accordance with your judgement, share the contents with the other Chapter Masters.'

Gage was still staring at the screen. He tapped one of the documents. As he read, his face turned grey. 'This contingency…' he began. His voice turned hoarse.

'None can be excluded,' Guilliman said. 'I would betray my mission if I did.'

'But…'

'The Ultramarines are more than any of us. They are more than me too.'

Gage shook his head.

'Oh? Did the Thirteenth Legion not exist before my Father found me?'

'Not truly,' Gage said. 'We only thought we did. And now we know who we are…'

'You will always know,' Guilliman finished for him. 'I swear it.' He smiled. 'I have no intention of dying. I have far too much to do.'

'No,' said Gage. 'No.' He held the slate at arm's length as if it were diseased.

'Every eventuality must be confronted,' Guilliman told him. 'To do otherwise is a betrayal.'

'Has the Emperor?'

The absurdity of the question almost made Guilliman laugh. Gage was more distressed than he had expected. He waited for Gage to realise what he had just asked.

At last the Chapter Master Primus lowered his arm. He looked down at the slate. He said nothing.

'The culture of the Ultramarines must be as much a living thing as the Imperium,' Guilliman said. 'It must be the bedrock of every legionary's strength, and the lifeblood of every Chapter, company and squad.'

'Do you understand what you're asking us to envision?' Gage asked.

Guilliman frowned. 'I was under the impression *I* was trying to make *you* understand.'

'Osiris,' Gage said. 'The losses we suffered there almost carved the heart out of the Legion.'

'I know.'

Gage held up the data-slate for a moment. 'What you contemplate here is infinitely worse than what happened on Septus Twelve. When Lord Commander Vosotho was killed by the psybrids, the Legion was decapitated. How can those of us who were there even think of revisiting that trauma? And Vosotho was our leader, not our primarch. We didn't know we had one, then. As for our brothers who came after, they don't even have the knowledge of having survived Osiris to sustain them. We can't go back to that pain. We won't.'

'That's right,' Guilliman said. 'You won't. Why do you think I'm talking about our culture? Those documents are not thought games or exercises designed to torment you. I can't pretend I will live forever. I will not be derelict in *my* duty to the Legion and to my Father. I can't ensure my eternal existence. I will do everything in my power to ensure the Legion's. The Ultramarines *will* be forever. You are my sons. You are my essence. So is the Legion, and what animates it.' He swept his arm to take in the manuscripts and notes on the desk, and the volumes stacked and classified in the high bookcases on the walls adjoining the crystalflex. 'I live in these words. I live in the thoughts they embody. This is more than my legacy. This is me.' He took a step towards Gage. 'I will shape the Ultramarines into what they must be. Duty compels us all, Marius, and that is mine. My duty is the destiny of the Legion.'

He paused. He tried to see the effect of his words on Gage. The Chapter Master Primus was nodding, slowly, still grim of face. *Good*, Guilliman thought. *He sees.*

'What I am asking you to face is no different, in essence, from what I demanded today of Iasus and the Twenty-second. Iasus will correct the course of the Chapter. He will make it a full partner in the culture of the Legion. And that,' he said, pointing to the slate in Gage's hand, 'is the guarantor of continuity.'

Gage said, 'I won't fail you, primarch. None of us will.'

'I know you won't.' Once again he thought, *Good*. 'Then let's bring the impact of our culture to the greenskins.'

Gage was a fraction of a second slow to begin to follow, as if his mind were somewhere back in the paths of their conversation. Guilliman looked back. The old warrior's face was set, grim, and determined. The shadow of an old grief hovered over him.

The shadow of a future one seemed to stretch before him.

Recursion: the theoretical and the practical are the keys to their own reinforcement. Theoretical: the full implementation of the theoretical and the practical is the means by which their strength achieves its most complete realisation. Practical: instillation, through edict and usage, of the theoretical and practical at every level, and at every instance, even and especially including those situations where the correct course of action appears self-evident. It is these moments that provide the greatest risks and opportunities. The obvious is treacherous, thus doubly in need of rigorous interrogation. The application of the theoretical and practical in these instances thus reinforces the approach for all other circumstances.

– Guilliman, *Towards a Union of Theory and Praxis,* 111.54.xl

THREE

INSIGHT • POTENTIAL • ACTUAL

The *Cavascor*'s deck vibrated. Hierax felt it through the soles of his boots. It was the pulse of the launches. The heartbeat of the strike cruiser had become the drum of war.

He was on the bridge. The rest of the 22nd Chapter was descending to Thoas while the Destroyers, once more, remained in orbit, their strength chained, their way of war denied. Iasus had given the order. Perhaps he had come to the decision on his own. It was very possible. He had been given his position for a reason. Ultimately, though, it was Guilliman's distaste for what the Destroyers were and did that held them at bay.

Hierax had come to the bridge to watch, and to be seen. The situation of the Destroyers was known across the Chapter's ships. That they were again denied the battlefield was not a source of shame. Nonetheless, the frustration of the companies translated into tension and discontent throughout the Chapter. He had spoken with Laches, whose First Destroyers were stationed on the frigate *Glory of Fire*. Laches was on the bridge there too. The captains were in position, to observe and stand ready, and to present the unbowed pride of the companies.

Hierax was in the strategium, standing in the pulpit. It

projected forwards into the space of the bridge. He was visible to
every officer, serf and technician. He emanated a sculpted calm
as he watched the oculus and listened to the launch reports.
He gave his full attention to the deployment. He would watch
and study every step of this war. He and his company would
be ready the instant an order to deploy came.

Bootsteps sounded behind him. He turned. Legionary Kletos had entered the strategium. His armour, like that of all
Destroyers, was predominantly black. With the departure of
the other companies, the only Legiones Astartes heraldry still
visible aboard the Nemesis Chapter ships was the dark of unfor-
giving, brutal, scorching war.

The colours of necessity, Hierax thought. *We do not engage without reason. But we cannot be ignored or forgotten. War forbids it.*

Kletos saluted. 'You wanted to see me, captain,' he said.

Hierax nodded. 'I'm taking a sounding, legionary. How would
you describe the mood in the ranks?'

Kletos cocked his head. He was not wearing his helmet, and
he made no attempt to moderate his expression. He had been
badly burned in the hive on Septus XII when the psybrids had
sprung their trap. His face was a mass of glistening scar tissue.
Unlike Hierax's wounds, which had accumulated over the length
of his career, the mark of Kletos' injury had come all at once. The
right corner of his mouth was pulled down, making him appear
perpetually sardonic. Which was not that far from the truth.

'With due respect, captain,' Kletos said, 'I think you can guess.'

'I choose not to.'

Kletos shrugged. 'Right. Ugly, then.'

And this was why Hierax had called on Kletos. The legionary
was plain-spoken to a fault. He balanced on the razor's edge
of insubordination with such regularity, he would never make
sergeant. As a barometer of the company's mood, he could not
be bettered.

'Uglier than the last time?'

'I should say so.'

'And the difference is…'

Kletos snorted. 'The Chapter Master.'

Hierax lowered his voice. 'Go on.'

Kletos took the hint and spoke softly, for Hierax's ears alone. 'He's wrong for us. He's an outsider several times over. Might as well be from another Legion.'

'How bad is it?'

'Bad enough. If he tries to change us into something we're not…' Kletos trailed off.

'If he tries, then what?' Hierax said, his voice harsh.

Kletos cursed. 'I don't know. No one does. We can't stop him, so we'll resent him even more.'

'The discussion is that involved already?'

'Yes.'

Theoreticals without practicals, Hierax thought. The insight struck him as important, but he could not see what to do with it. *No practical for me either.*

What he could see was an immediate danger. Resentment bred mistakes. 'The talk,' he said. 'How widespread is it? Does it reach beyond the company?'

Kletos nodded. 'I was speaking to some brothers in the 223rd. They're no happier. I've heard rumblings from other companies too.'

The more Kletos spoke, the more Hierax's personal anger was mixed with concern. He had been thinking of the long-term transformation of the Chapter when he had spoken with Sirras. That long term was clearly troubling the rank and file too. But it was the short term that worried him now. Resentment over the time ahead could jeopardise the present.

'Reassure our brothers,' Hierax told Kletos. 'We will always be who we are.'

'Oh? How?'

'Are you doubting my word, legionary?'

'Just curious. As they will be.'

He dodged the question. 'If an identity can be altered so easily, it isn't worth preserving in the first place.'

'Of course,' said Kletos. The corner of his mouth twitched down even further.

'That will be all,' Hierax said.

Kletos saluted and left the strategium. Hierax turned back to the oculus, and the display of the great plain on Thoas. Engine flares and the heat streaks of drop pods burned through the atmosphere. Already the first mobilisations would be occurring in the western reaches of the plain. And in the east, the orks would be stirring. He did not need any augur readings to tell him that. He could read the patterns of the war's birth without seeing them.

The thoughts of the Nemesis Chapter's morale ate at him. His hope, in observing the war, was to find the opportunity to prove to Guilliman the need for the Destroyers. Deployment and vindication – they would create the path out of his festering resentment. They would be the salvation for a Chapter that he did not believe needed to be saved from itself by an outsider.

Now, though, his hope receded before the dread his talk with Kletos had fed. The risk did not lie with the Destroyers, held far from combat. It lay with the rest of the Chapter, no less bitter but deployed in the field. Where the mistakes could happen.

'Theoretical...' he murmured. *Resentment in troops is a force multiplier for errors.* 'Practical...' *Deploy them to see what happens.*

With an effort of will, he went no further down that mental path. The speculation was unproductive. It was also, he knew, unnecessary. The theoretical's truth or falsity would be manifest soon enough.

He turned his attention from the oculus to the pict screens in the strategium. He watched the lengthening columns of company runes and landing coordinates. He tried to focus on the expanding minutiae of the landings, to fill his mind with the effort of visualising the countless vectors of the action below.

Despite his efforts, the questions he wanted to avoid rose, dragged to the surface by the very chain of logic the primarch had instilled in his sons. If Hierax wanted Guilliman to see how vital the Destroyers were, it followed that Guilliman was blind to that truth. Was he then blind to the consequences of Iasus' appointment?

If so, what else might he not be seeing?

This is your anger speaking, Hierax tried to tell himself.

He had never been good at lying to himself.

War was thunder, and there were as many forms of warfare as there were kinds of thunder. Guilliman knew them well. He could tell, from the rhythm, timbre and beat of the roar, the nature of the combatants and the state of the clash. What he heard was not cacophony. He heard the language of battle, the world-shaking argument and counter-argument of a debate drenched in blood, embraced by flame. He knew all the articulations of strike and retaliation. Most of all, he knew the thunder of his Legion.

Guilliman stood in the open hatch of Land Raider Proteus *Flame of Illyrium*. Inside the hull, the Invictarii honour guard waited to be unleashed. Guilliman drank in the thunder of the gathering strength of the Ultramarines. This was the thunder of preparation, of a potential building up until it must be unleashed, a fist that could topple mountains.

It would be easy to believe the sound alone could flatten all before it. The sky trembled, battered by the constant roar of descending transports, heavy lifters and gunships. As above, so below, and the ground trembled too. It shook beneath the treads of tanks, armoured carriers, and the march of thousands of ceramite boots. Guilliman looked up. The stars wavered, their light distorted by the contrails of arriving ships and the roil of dissipating promethium.

This far west of the cordillera, Thoas was dark with eternal night, cold with eternal winter. The plain was barren, its rocky protuberances worn down to smooth ripples as the superheated air of Thoas' day side rushed with unceasing monotony to the frigid night. There was heat in the winter now. The bones of the world were blasted by the flame of retro-firing engines. There was light too. It was the harsh gaze of landing lights and the targeting beams of tanks.

The tremors of the deployment travelled up the hull of *Flame of Illyrium*. Guilliman felt them through his gauntlets when he clutched the edge of the hatch. He breathed deeply of the sharp burn of spent fuel. And he listened to the thunder. It was the strength of his sons. It was the sound of the great machine of flesh and will, of discipline and steel, that was unfolding across the plain. It was the tectonic rumble of Thoas' reclamation. A force whose destructive power was unlimited, but whose purpose was, in the end, to purify and to build.

Your strength acts through me, Father, Guilliman thought. *Your will is mine. Let this world be part of the human supremacy once more.*

'...odd choice,' a voice was saying over the vox. It was Habron, in the driver's compartment of *Illyrium*.

'What is?' Guilliman asked the Techmarine.

'Thoas,' Habron repeated. '*The conditions of this world do not invite initial colonisation. Even less a full civilisation. How would it be sustained?*'

'Temperatures are still above freezing at the base of the mountains,' Guilliman said. The eastern end of the plain was within the terminator zone, held with the mountains in a permanent limbo, neither dawn nor twilight.

'*A narrow region,*' Habron objected. '*Hardly large enough to sustain a planetary population.*'

'Are you thinking of what was or what is to come?' Guilliman asked.

'*What is to come can be supplied,*' said Habron. '*What is past was isolated.*'

'Then we should look for answers in the ruins,' Guilliman said. 'Time, I think, that we reclaimed them.'

'*The Chapter Masters have signalled readiness.*'

'And the orks? Are they ready? Are they coming to greet us?'

He knew the answer. His choice of site for the deployment had been the result of rigorous calculation. It had to be close enough to the mountains for the orks to see the signs of descending ships. It had to be far enough away to give the Ultramarines the time and space to mobilise. The operating hypothesis was the orks would mobilise the instant they realised their hold on Thoas would be contested. The question was how quickly the orks would arrive.

'*They are,*' Habron confirmed. '*A moment, primarch. Updating.*'

There was silence for a few seconds while Habron used the explorator augury web. The Proteus' auspex sensor suite was Guilliman's sight where no sight was possible. It could peer through the walls of a fortress, pinpointing structural weakness and enemy concentrations. The orks were still too far away for the system to come into play, but Habron had linked the Explorator to the augurs and cogitators of the *Macragge's Honour*. The ship looked beyond the mustering zone's horizon to the advancing greenskins. The *Macragge's Honour* fed what it learned back to the *Flame of Illyrium*.

'*They are closing rapidly,*' Habron reported. '*They will be visible within the hour, assuming we hold position.*'

Which we won't, Guilliman thought. 'Can you give me a target?' he asked.

'*Large numbers of heat blooms. They have many vehicles…*'
Habron was quiet again for a moment. Guilliman waited without prompting him. '*Too many to make any determination at this stage,*' Habron said. '*The heat signatures have formed a single mass. I'll know more when I can use the Explorator's sensors directly.*'

'Then let us meet the foe.' Guilliman switched to the command channel of the vox to address the entire deployment. He climbed out of the hatch to stand on the roof of *Flame of Illyrium*. The Proteus was stationed at the easternmost edge of the landing zone.

'Warriors of the Thirteenth,' he called.

All eyes would be looking east now, towards the enemy, and towards the position where his legionaries knew he must be. He was visible to many, and even those too far away to catch sight of him would be gazing in this direction, sensing his presence with certainty. They were certain because of who he was, and how he had made himself known to them. Their genes were his. His being informed theirs. Their instincts flowed to the same purpose as his own. He was as his father had made him, and they were shaped to the same ends.

But what the Ultramarines knew in their blood, Guilliman had ensured was also a direct, conscious, ever-present truth. The Legion's command structure was predicated on the powerful commander. From the squad level on up, the leader gave more than direction. He shaped the battle. He was the pole star for his men, the figure of inspiration and the sign of the eternal advance. Every squad, every company, every Chapter was a series of vectors, all moving towards their individual goals, and each goal one aspect of the unified mission of the Legion. A multiplicity forged into a perfection of order.

Guilliman was the point of fusion. He was the fountainhead of command, and the confluence of goals. He was the leader who was as ultimate as he was necessary. On Macragge, before the coming of the Emperor, he had already embodied the role, but he did so as an unthinking part of his identity. It was only once he had taken command of the XIII, and undertaken to come to a full understanding of the connections between himself and his genetic sons, that he had articulated the theories of what he was and must be.

So now, at the dawn of another battle, he was the supreme commander, and he was the culminating symbol of command. He directed the movements of the Legion, and he was the ideal they looked to even when he was not physically present. Guilliman the symbol had a reality that surpassed Guilliman the physical being. That was as it should be. That was as he had designed. It was part of his great work.

His labour was far from done. There was another component to the integrity of command that was yet incomplete, and that he could not do alone. He needed Gage to face the realities of continuity. Gage was resistant. That was understandable. But he would do his duty, in time. They all would.

'Ultramarines!' Guilliman voxed. He raised the *Gladius Incandor*. The blade flashed silver, cold and pure as the stars of the Thoas night. 'The greenskins are approaching. March with me! We will meet them. We will purge them! We will return this planet to the human dominion!' He paused, and pointed *Incandor* at the horizon. 'The enemy's way of war is the way of the mob. Ours is the way of order. We fight with force, and we fight with reason, reason that is imbued in every decision and in every blow! We are the science and truth of war, and we will shatter the presumption of the foe! *We are honour and courage!*'

'*Honour and courage!*' The shout came from every throat in the Legion, and from every vox-speaker. It was the greatest thunder, rising above those of the hundreds of engines. It was the incarnation of the sublime. In a less secular age, he knew, what he heard would have been experienced as the roar of the Legion's soul.

As it was, his blood soared when his sons answered. He dropped back into the hatch, still standing, and faced the east, his lips pulled back in a grin of ferocious pride as the rumble of *Flame of Illyrium*'s engine became deafening. The tank surged forwards, a beast slipping its chain.

In the same moment, the Legion advanced. As the voices of his sons had taken up his war cry, now the gunships and transports and tanks answered the roar of *Illyrium*. The immense thunder that had shaken earth and sky as the Legion mustered now transcended itself. The individual warriors and vehicles joined together in a colossus of war. Guilliman did not like the concept of *perfection*. That was Fulgrim's obsession, and Guilliman doubted his brother would have seen fit to bestow that label on the Ultramarines advance. Guilliman had seen the look on Fulgrim's face during their joint operations. The approach of the XIII lacked finesse in his eyes. War for Fulgrim was an art. Strategy should be aesthetically pleasing as well as successful.

Guilliman thought it was enough for strategy to be sound. And for a Legion to be unstoppable.

The Ultramarines marched, and instead of *perfection*, there was *precision*. Guilliman prized that far above aesthetics. *Precision and rigour*. War was not an art. It was a science. It was the application of overwhelming force with the full consciousness of where and how and why. Art could come in the wake of war. Art belonged in the creation and reconstruction that were the true ends of war's means. Success in war was to bring it to a swift and complete end.

Behind Guilliman, stretching off as far as he could see to the left and right on the plain, the Legion's strength advanced so implacably, it was as if a tectonic plate were going to war. Guilliman breathed in the roiling smoke of hundreds of engines.

He took in the flash and burst of vehicle lamps, and the glow of gunship engines. The Ultramarines had brought the light of the human galaxy to the surface of Thoas.

He turned his eyes to the horizon and voxed Habron. 'How fast is the enemy approaching?'

'*Still accelerating,*' Habron said after a moment. '*And variable across the horde.*' He read off a group of figures and the average speed of the leading edge of the greenskin army.

Guilliman calculated the rate of advance of the two forces. He gazed hard into the east. The promise of dawn glimmered there. It would never arrive. One did not wait for dawn on Thoas. It had to be hunted. And the Legion was heading its way. The orks, though, were not as implacable as the unmoving sun, no matter how much they deluded themselves about their strength and power. They had already been dislodged from their high ground. They could be made to move. They were rushing to the night, and to their oblivion.

He would see them very soon.

Guilliman used the moments that remained to vox Gage.

'What do you see, Marius?' he asked.

'*What do you want me to see?*'

Gage wasn't fooled by the question. He knew Guilliman was not asking whether he had spotted the foe.

'I see our Legion,' Guilliman told him.

'*As do I.*'

'Do you see its shape? I don't mean the formations. I mean what they signify.'

A pause. '*The theoretical given practical form,*' Gage said.

'Yes,' said Guilliman. 'And in this moment, the practical made theoretical. That's the paradox of the march to battle. Can you see it? We have lost nothing. The formations are flawless. Our strength is at its greatest potential. This is the perfection of the moment before battle.' He said *perfection* deliberately. The embodied potential was an ideal, one that would encounter reality and instantly transform. This was something he didn't think Fulgrim would ever understand. Guilliman had certainly never been able to make his brother see the impossibility of his quest. Fulgrim believed the ideal could exist in battle, and he pursued its manifestation. Guilliman knew what happened to ideals. 'We must never be blinded by the aesthetic magnificence of the purely theoretical,' he told Gage. 'Just like we cannot let ourselves be defined by the brute calculation of the solely practical. The practical grounds the dreams of the theoretical. The theoretical gives flight to the realities of the practical.'

'*Always*,' Gage said.

'Yes. Always.' Even in the heat of battle, and at the smallest level of the Legion's organisation. The possible and the actual worked in symbiosis, and in their fusion was victory. That was more valuable than the pursuit of the unattainable. Fulgrim performed wonders chasing that goal, but Guilliman wondered what satisfaction he found in that. All he could imagine was eternal frustration.

Observation. Analysis. Determination. Execution. That cycle repeated until it led to a victory that had all the appearance of being inevitable. And perhaps it was: preordained by the XIII Legion's philosophical machine of war.

There was real satisfaction in that cycle. If Guilliman felt hunger, it was in the desire for the cycle's continued adaptation and adjustment. The endless lessons he learned assuaged that hunger, then pushed him towards its greater consideration, and a new implementation. He did not seek perfection. The process was its own fulfilment.

'*Lord Guilliman*,' Habron voxed.

'I know,' Guilliman answered. He saw the change at the horizon.

The boundary between land and sky was visible as an uneven

line of deeper black beneath the firmament. The glitter of the stars ended, cut off by contours of eroded rock. Now the line moved and blurred. A huge mass was coming into view. Then there was light. It was ugly, smoky, crude, the belched flame of burning fuel and exploding fumes. It was, Guilliman thought, not true light at all. Savagery could illuminate nothing. It was the fire of barbarism, and nothing more. But it revealed the enemy.

The clamour of the orks came on before them. Carried by the perpetual west wind, the howling came from hundreds of thousands of animalistic maws and from the grinding of engines so crude they should have already been destroyed by catastrophic malfunctions. Guilliman's ear separated the roar of the orks from the roar of the Ultramarines. It was the difference between destructive instinct and purpose-led order. The difference between the monstrosity of the past and the infinite hope of the future.

The armies raced towards each other. The brutish shrieking of the enemy became ecstatic as the orks caught sight of the Ultramarines.

'*Someone should tell them they've lost their empire,*' Gage said.

'I doubt they even know what they had,' said Guilliman. The greenskins understood battle and the joy of pillage. He doubted their comprehension extended much beyond the frenzy of the moment. They were worthy foes if all one sought was the contest of strength. But they did not have true empires. They were infestations that spread across worlds. The Ultramarines had quarantined this particular multi-system disease. Now they were going to wipe out the final infection.

'Do you have targets for us yet?' Guilliman asked Habron.

'*Resolving them now,*' Habron said. As the greenskin horde came into sight, the Proteus' Explorator cast the gaze of its scanners over the army. Cognis-interpreters read movements, picked up on the currents that portended localised surges, and evaluated the points of disruption.

Guilliman already knew the kind of target the Explorator would select. He had already done so. What he wanted was the coordinates. The augur system's eyes were still better than his. They ranged much further.

'*Found them,*' Habron said. '*Multiple vehicle clusters converging on a point directly ahead of our position.*'

Guilliman nodded. *Flame of Illyrium* was leading a great column projecting out from the main force of the Ultramarines. The column was the spear tip. It was also the bait. The orks saw it first. There was no coordination in their attack. It was a colossal wave, stretching north and south far beyond Guilliman's sight, far wider than the span of the XIII Legion formations. The wave was a mass of individuals. Every brute fought on its own terms. The orks triumphed over organised armies through numbers and crude strength. An illusion of strategy occurred when a large mob of raging individuals all chose the same target at once.

Guilliman had given them their target so they would reveal to him what he sought.

Theoretical: the enemy can be made to conform to the battlefield. Practical: this enemy knows only direct battle against the most visible target. Offer that target in controlled conditions, and you shape the encounter.

'*I have coordinates for the largest concentration,*' Habron said.

'Relay them,' Guilliman said. Over the command channel he voxed, 'Gunships and artillery, you have your data. Fire at will.'

The Basilisk and Whirlwind tanks began their attack first. A new order of thunder shook the land. Flights of vengeance missiles flashed overhead, their blazing contrails tearing open the curtain of night. A terrible, strobing day lit the plain, turning the stony ground into a jagged mosaic of bleached white and knife-edged shadows. The deeper booms of the earthshaker cannons of the Basilisks followed.

Guilliman glanced back to see the rows of barrels flare. He nodded, satisfied by the precision he saw, the rhythm of fire calculated to cause maximum damage to the enemy. He looked forwards again. From just over the horizon, deep in the midst of the orks, the fireballs blossomed, first in a rapid accumulation as the missiles hit. Then the shells of the earthshakers came down, and their explosions were majestic. The blasts continued to multiply, spreading out from the initial target sites. Burning wreckage marched over the orks as their vehicles, too close together and too volatile, detonated.

The Thunderhawks streaked over the orks. Heavy bombs fell from their pylon mounts. Violent dawn erupted from the core of the horde. Explosions radiated outwards from the centre of the targeted area. The night pulled back from the billowing, bellowing flame. The devastation already spread over a region hundreds of yards on a side. The gunships pulled away, and the artillery tanks fired again.

Guilliman saw the impact of his first blow take hold as *Flame of Illyrium* travelled over the final distance separating the Ultramarines from the orks. The Legion's advance was sure, unbroken, a battering ram of Imperial technology. The wave of the orks foundered on the reef of a high-explosive barrage. Only a small portion of the green tide had been struck, but the effect was widespread. The burning vehicles created a lethal barrier before the onrushing brutes. The orks in the lead turned in confusion as the battle suddenly seemed to have moved to their midst.

This much, Guilliman could see or extrapolate from the wall of flames rising in the near distance. 'Update,' he said to Habron. There was time for one more before the furnace of combat. The horde was like a huge, turbulent river. It had direction, yet the undisciplined movement of the mob created flows within of different speeds. He needed to know how the ork currents further out – the ones in the night, beyond the reach of the flames – were reacting.

'*Disorder in the currents*,' Habron reported. '*The more distant portions of the horde are trying to push forwards towards the explosions. They're placing pressure on the centre. Forward momentum is greatly reduced. There is very little coherence at this time.*'

'Good.' On the command channel he said, 'Theoretical – use the orks against themselves. Practical – lure them into a semblance of order, then disrupt it. The rewards of our way of war await! Courage and honour!'

He heard the war cry again at the same moment the sponson-mounted lascannons of the Proteus fired. The energy beams cut across the narrowing stretch of land that separated the Ultramarines from the orks. Across the width of the column, tanks poured las and heavy bolter shells into the enemy. Further back, the other Chapters in the broader phalanx held their fire. They closed in on the orks, an immense force ignored by the enemy.

The Proteus' las-beams burned a path through the orks. Guilliman climbed out of the hatch. He crouched on *Illyrium*'s roof. His left hand still held *Incandor*. His right unlocked the *Arbitrator* from his belt. His finger curled around the ornate trigger of the combi-bolter. He waited for the tactical moment to leap from the tank, to extend the force of the phalanx with his personal strength.

There were new stenches in the air now. There was the cloying, foul animal musk of the greenskins. It was a biological aggression so sharp it sliced through the clouds of promethium. And there was the smell of burned flesh. Already many hundreds of greenskins had been blown apart and incinerated. The cloud of their death reached its tendrils across the plain.

The leading column of the Ultramarines plunged into the

uproar of the enemy. The leading edge of the blade, the gladius stab into the orks, was still a thousand yards wide. Two rows of heavy armour came first, blasting greenskins to cinders and scraping them to bloody smears on the land with their siege blades. Behind the tanks came the legionaries of the First Chapter. The sea of orks milled and howled, pushed back, crushed and blown apart. But it truly was a sea, and the surge of roaring bodies, swollen with muscle and rage, crashed forwards again.

The greenskins fired crude projectile firearms and wielded mis-shapen blades heavy enough to cut through steel. They were as confused as they were wrathful, and so it was the sheer crush of numbers that hurled them against the XIII Legion. Their attack lacked the force of their full charge. They ran into regimented bolter fire and a synchrony of chainswords. The companies marched into the wall of flesh. They cut the brutes down. They expanded the blade wound.

Instinct and anger urged the orks to destroy the enemy that had come into their midst. If they turned their eyes to the west and saw what was coming, either they ignored it for the immediate foe, or they did not understand the immensity of what they beheld.

'The currents of the horde are still confused,' Habron reported. 'We are the centre of what focus they are managing.'

On the roof of *Illyrium*, Guilliman straightened. He held *Incandor* aloft, its silver flash a challenge to the orks and a beacon to his sons. He sprayed a wide arc of the ground before the Proteus with the double-timed hammering of his shells. Mass-reactive warheads punched into the bodies of the greenskins and exploded. They vaporised blood. They turned bone into shrapnel. Fountains of ruptured flesh and xenos blood sprayed upwards on all sides of the Proteus. It rained down on Guilliman. His face was soaked with the death of the foe. The roar of guns overwhelmed the roar of the orks.

A good start, Guilliman thought. *A good first blow*. Smoke covered the battlefield. He breathed it in. It rasped against the back of his throat. He savoured the taste of a falling enemy.

The first seconds of the clash belonged to the Ultramarines.

Guilliman kept firing. The orks died, and more rushed forwards. *Flame of Illyrium* bucked upwards as it climbed over a growing mound of bodies.

The deafening chorus of snarls changed tone. The orks were finding their direction again. The crush of numbers became a focused counter-attack. They ceased to care about the barrage tearing apart their centre. They wanted the legionaries. They wanted prey they could rip apart. The individual challenge roared by thousands upon thousands of bestial voices became a ferocious unity. In phalanxes a hundred-strong, the Ultramarines marched into the orks. But their advance began to slow. The orks lost their confusion.

Guilliman looked right and cursed. It was too late to help as the squad of Sergeant Tibron was overwhelmed by dozens of greenskins. The orks leapt right into the bolter fire. The leading brutes went down while their fellows lunged closer. The legionaries couldn't cut the orks down fast enough. A huge beast slumped forwards, its chest blown out. It grabbed at its killer as if fell and knocked the barrel down. The ork behind jumped over the dying greenskin. It raised a chainaxe over its head in midair. It brought the weapon down, smashing open Tibron's helmet and cleaving his skull in two. Beside him, two of his brothers disappeared under an avalanche of immense xenos bodies.

'Maintain course,' Guilliman ordered Habron. 'Invictarii, with me.' He leapt from the roof of the tank. The side hatches banged open, unleashing the honour guard on the greenskins.

Guilliman fired into the orks. He shredded them with bolter fire. He and the Invictarii waded into their midst, drawing their attack and taking them apart while the squad regrouped. Guilli-man blasted the orks coming from the forward position. To his left, he jabbed *Incandor* through the forehead of another green-skin. The thick bones cracked like an eggshell from the force of his blow. The blade sliced through the ork's brain. He pulled the gladius out and stabbed again, killing another ork before the body of the first had hit the ground.

'They think they have our measure!' Guilliman called to the Legion. 'Instead we have theirs!'

Ahead, a clanking behemoth crashed through the wreckage barrier. Gears screamed in their eagerness to prove Guilliman wrong.

The great pitfall of observation and analysis is assumption. Guard against it. The very rigour of thought lends strength to the temptation. Pride and consciousness of the knowing application of the science of warfare opens the mind to the hubris of infallibility. Assumptions result, and mistakes inevitably follow. The shield against such potentially fatal battlefield errors is adaptability. This is not simply – or even principally – the physical resilience that permits survival in adverse, shifting conditions. It is the ability to recognise that a given theoretical is exactly that: theoretical. Contrary facts must be respected, and the theory must be altered, or even abandoned, as indicated by reality, not by desire. The practical and war are both fluid and evolving. The advantage of the practical is that it is also conscious.

– Guilliman, *Prologomena to Tactics,* 10.4.iii

FOUR

THE PLAIN • STRONGPOINT • EVERYWHERE

The vehicle was a monstrous creation of chance. Anything the orks managed to construct that was more complex than their axes and cleavers seemed to Guilliman to be the result more of happenstance than will. The question of how they managed to construct even a single void-worthy craft was still a mystery, one that had consumed the thoughts of more than one remembrancer.

Even at first glance, Guilliman could easily imagine how this creation had come to pass. It looked like two separate vehicles had collided in the late stages of their construction. Its core was bulbous, as if still swelling from the force of the impact. Plates overlapped and folded against each other. The thing had too many wheels. Its shape was a sprawling nightmare. Its axles were bent. Some of the wheels were turned, at odds with the direction of the majority. Limbs projected from the fused chassis. They carried chains, wrecking balls and six-foot blades. Larger projectile guns than the ones carried by the foot soldiers were mounted on a multitude of skewed turrets.

The thing wasn't a tank. It wasn't a transport. The orks had been building two of their attack trucks, and the collision had, instead of destroying both, created a thing that still functioned. The orks had built upon their chance machine, adding more and more guns and assault arms, slapping armour plate atop of armour plate. Now it bristled with death and the feral pride of the brutes.

It appeared, and all the orks within sight of the creation shouted in joyous ferocity. It was a mad thing, and its mere existence was their promise of ecstatic battle.

It must die, Guilliman thought. It was an engine of ork morale. It had to be removed from the field.

The vehicle was two hundred yards north-east of his position. It would pass him by unless he caught up to it.

The Land Raider *Ozirus* closed with it, lascannons and heavy bolters pounding the front armour. Turrets exploded. Flames raced over the hull of the vehicle. It kept going. Guilliman counted at least six turrets still active. Their fire burst against the armour of *Ozirus*.

The two vehicles rumbled past each other. The ork machine's huge wrecking balls slammed into the flank of the Land Raider. The tank's composite held. But one of the huge masses hit the port sponson. It crushed the barrels of the lascannons as they fired. The guns exploded, damaging the armour in a way the ork vehicle could never have managed with its own weaponry. Energy blasted back into the Land Raider, triggering reserves of energy cells. The flash of the guns became a blinding, uncontrolled discharge. The port flank of *Ozirus* blew out. The wreckage slammed into the ork machine, collapsing that side of its hull. The vehicle barrelled on. It was excess given metallic form. It should never have worked at all, and because it did, it was unstoppable.

Behind it came more ork vehicles, belching clouds of black smoke, streams of flame bursting from exhaust pipes and from between the seams of the poorly welded iron plates. The initial bombardment had destroyed many of the machines the orks were capable of fielding. Some had survived, though, and they had gathered behind the largest. They converged on the wounded *Ozirus*. Their solid shells slammed into it. Most bounced off the forward armour, but some found the huge rent in the port flank. The Land Raider was still moving, sluggishly, and fired only from the starboard side.

Guilliman pounded over the ground towards *Ozirus*. He ran alone, leaving the Invictarii behind to continue cutting the path forwards through the horde. The risk was a strategic one. *Theoretical: the greatest blow to ork morale will be a single warrior destroying their great weapon. Practical: I must be that warrior.* He fired as he ran, blasting the way clear through the brutes. The orks came at him with all their muscular savagery. Some of the beasts were almost twice his height. He did not let them slow him. He blew them apart with the shells of the *Arbitrator*. *Incandor* slashed throats and cut torsos wide open. He was a blade. His route took him through the bodies of his foe, reaping a tidal surge of blood.

He was less than fifty feet from the stricken Land Raider. The ork machines had it surrounded. There were dozens of the vehicles. They were beyond crude. They were all accidents of design; products of savage enthusiasm that functioned despite themselves, explosive agglomerations of aggression and industry. They had isolated *Ozirus* from the other Ultramarines tanks. A pair of Land Raiders was blowing up the outlier ork machines, trying to force their way back in to aid *Ozirus*. The others had no choice but to continue the advance. Guilliman had ordered there be no gap in the exterminating wall of heavy armour. The march must not stop. The orks were disorder and riot. They would be driven back and purged from Thoas by discipline and coherent strategy.

There were costs to order. *Ozirus* might be one. But Guilliman had the freedom of movement. Where he moved in the field, he created the means of the advance.

Thirty feet. Orks were jumping off the crowded roofs and sides of their vehicles and rushing into the gap in the Land Raider. They were mowed down by the fire of their own turrets and by the resistance of the Ultramarines in the tank. But there were always more.

Fifteen feet. *Ozirus* exploded. The fireball was sudden, a gigantic blast of killing light. Guilliman ran into the shock wave. Heat and force tried to scorch the flesh from his skull. Slabs of twisted armour wheeled end over end past him. Guilliman kept moving, straight into the fire, straight into the furnace. There was a moment when the world disappeared. He moved through a cauldron of deafening white pain. He pushed through it, carried by momentum and anger, and most of all by necessity. On the other side was the blackened, roaring hulk of the ork machine. It was charging forwards again, multiple engines screaming with eagerness for more prey.

Guilliman leapt.

The arc of his jump carried him to the roof of the machine. It was a forest of pipes and turrets and spikes. He came down through a hail of shells. Flame and smoke billowed around him. The orks riding the vehicle saw him coming.

That did them no good. No preparation could help them. He landed with a blow that resonated through the entire hull. An ork died beneath his boots, its back crushed to pulp. The plating on the roof cracked and bent inwards. The vehicle shuddered. Its advance hesitated.

Guilliman made his way towards the rear, where the hull bulged and a forest of pipes spewed flame into the night. Greenskins clambered over the roof after him. He blasted them with the *Arbitrator*. The impact of the shells sent their bodies flying from the vehicle. He sheathed *Incandor* and wrapped his gauntlet around the nearest pipe. He squeezed. He wasn't wearing the *Hand of Dominion*, but he didn't need the power gauntlet. His own strength was more than enough. He constricted one pipe after another, forcing the heat flow back inside the engine. By the time he reached the back of the vehicle, the roof was trembling from the pressure. A loose exhaust pipe shot off like a missile. A jet of flame screamed upwards in its wake.

Guilliman fired downwards. The combi-bolter's shells hit the armour like a focused artillery strike. They punched through the metal and into the furnace of the engine. Guilliman kept firing. Orks howled and clawed over each other in an effort to reach him and pull him down. Without shifting his focus, he grabbed *Incandor* from its maglocked belt sheath. In the corner of his eye, he saw the shapes come for him and he ripped them open. He was immobile, absolute as a mountain. The ork machine lurched forwards. It veered left and right as if it might shake him off. He kept shooting into the engine, pummelling the interior with a directed stream of explosions. The orks shrieked with frustration. Bullets careened off his armour. Blows landed. They meant nothing. He was unmoved.

He was the judgement of reason, and he brought destruction to the unthinking war of the beasts.

Guilliman felt the engines go critical. The hull tremors became violent and erratic, a heart in fibrillation. He jumped again, off the rear of the vehicle. He landed in the midst of more orks. He was killing again as the machine rumbled and juddered away from him. The clanking of its mechanism turned into the screech of tearing metal. The greenskins aboard ignored him now. They wailed as they fought to preserve the giant engine. Their efforts were futile. They did not understand how they had made their wonder. They knew even less how to preserve it.

The machine exploded. Its death was even more violent than

that of *Ozirus*. It was as if all the brute energy of the species had been contained within the hull, and now it was unleashed in a single gigantic blast. The explosion formed a crater. Fire, earth, wind and metal slammed into Guilliman. It flattened the orks around him. It burned them. A chunk of shrapnel larger than a man sailed past him and cut a greenskin in half. Guilliman rooted himself. He turned his face from the explosion, but stood fast in the holocaust. Before the light faded, he heard another deep-throated explosion, and then another. The destruction of the vehicle was so huge it had reached the machines that had followed it so closely. They died for clinging to the irrational logic of survivors. They had clustered with the perceived victor, and now they perished.

The firestorm spread. It gathered strength. Guilliman had avenged the killing of *Ozirus* and its crew, but that was not enough. This instant was another moment to seize.

All plans must adapt to contingent realities, or they are not plans. They are dreams.

'All units open fire!' he voxed to the other Chapters. The battle was only a few minutes old, and the leading phalanx had still not fully plunged into the green tide. But this moment must be amplified. 'Choose your enemies and destroy them. Artillery, we have more vehicular concentration. Target my coordinates. I want a massive bombardment *now*.'

He shouted from deep within the firestorm. He could barely hear his own voice in the blank thunder of the flames. But he heard the new thunder when it came. He heard the shrieking of the shells. And he heard the shattering percussion of the shells landing. He strode through the devastation, killing the few orks that managed to withstand the gunship cluster bombs and the earthshaker ordnance. He moved through the blasts, listening for the roar of Thunderhawk engines and the whistle of descending shells, his hearing so fine he knew where the explosives would fall. He moved back and forth across the fiery plain, wrapped in the storm he had summoned.

He emerged from the destruction. He left behind a new graveyard of ork vehicles. Ahead, the companies of the First Chapter kept faith with the strategy and continued to plough a thousand-yard-wide furrow through the orks. Guilliman stormed forwards, *Incandor* held high. He passed through one company after another, joining his sons in the purging slaughter, and when they saw him, they shouted to him, and tore into the enemy with redoubled fury.

Onwards, from company to company, until he was leading again, marching ahead of the line of tanks, scything the orks with gladius and shell.

Always advancing. This was the coherence of a battle with no ground yet to hold. Always towards the east, towards the mountains.

Towards the ruins, bringing the new glory of humanity to reclaim the old.

The orks were still fighting to reach the phalanx of the First Chapter when the rest of the Legion reached them. The line of the advance went from a thousand yards wide to ten times that. The orks covered an even greater area, but they had taken Guilliman's bait. They were concentrated but focused on the wrong target. The main attack of the Ultramarines swept over them like a volcanic blast. Sirras ran with his command squad between and just ahead of the Land Raiders, leading the 223rd's destruction of the orks. He thought of Hierax on the *Cavascor*. He wished for his old friend's presence. The opening moments of the campaign were deeply satisfying. The extermination of the enemy would be complete, even without the Destroyers' weapons. The final end of this ork empire was preordained, and Hierax deserved his share of the glory.

An hour later, Sirras was wishing for Hierax's arsenal. The orks shook off the impact of the initial shock. They were still dying, and the Ultramarines were still advancing through them. But the orks were not fighting a defensive war. They didn't care about positions or held territory. All that mattered to them was the battle itself. They hurled themselves against the XIII Legion formations, but they also pulled back and circled around for a new angle of attack. There were so many of them, they attacked and retreated simultaneously. The contradictory movements were just eddies and currents in the green sea.

Sirras took apart a hulking chieftain with his lightning claws, then jumped on top of his command Rhino *Eknomos* for a better vantage of the battlefield. He looked back. He saw the orks flooding around the rear of his company, opening up another front there. The advance suddenly meant nothing. Wherever he looked, there were greenskins beyond counting. The artillery barrage and the actions of the First Chapter had destroyed virtually all of what passed for ork heavy armour. But the enemy's numbers had not been affected at all.

Cursing, he turned around, surveying the battlefield. The 22nd Chapter was operating at the northernmost edge of the Ultramarines front. To the north, there was nothing but orks, and also to the west, as if the Legion had never passed through. To the east, with orks now visibly pouring down their slopes, the mountains were closer, along with the endless twilight. Above, the sky was already lighter, the stars more dim. To the south, the upheaval of war, the companies of twelve Chapters turning the plain into a vista of smoke and fire and blood. There Sirras saw the illusion of progress. The orks hit the forward edge of the companies, and the primarch's great engine of war ground them to mulch. No ork attacking from the east was alive by the time the last battle-brothers marched over the point of initial contact.

It was all illusion, Sirras thought. The orks had an inexhaustible supply of warriors. The mob descended mountainsides along a line at least ten miles long. The entire span of the Chapters was no more than the central portion of the greenskin wave. Tens of thousands of orks could not enter the war from the front, and so they looped around. The battles at the rear of the companies were already ferocious, and they were slowing down the pace of the advance as a whole.

They've surrounded us, Sirras thought. *They'll try to drown us.*

He refused to accept the possibility of defeat. Instead, he looked for the means to prevent it.

He looked north again. The land sloped away gradually in that direction. His gaze stopped on a deep shadow. It was much darker than the others cast over the plain by the mountains. It was long and jagged, its edges sharply defined. And the orks were going around it.

Sirras blinked through levels of magnification of his helmet's photolenses. The shadow was a chasm in the plain, a narrow canyon, perhaps five hundred yards across at its widest. Its nearest point was less than a mile away.

There were ways of ensuring what fell into those depths never emerged.

He opened the Rhino's hatch and dropped inside. Techmarine Nicandrus looked up from the banks of command screens and auspex arrays. 'I want a topographical scan,' Sirras told him. 'North, approximately two thousand yards from our position.'

He stood over Nicandrus and watched the image appear, layer by layer on the pict screen. The gorge was a deep one. The sides were close to the vertical. 'A unique feature in this area,' Nicandrus said.

'One to be exploited,' said Sirras. He opened a vox-channel to Iasus. 'Chapter Master,' he said, 'we have an opportunity. I propose to take the 223rd north of our current position to force the orks into a canyon.' The correct manoeuvre could doom thousands of the greenskins. And the gorge was a real barrier to their movements.

'*Negative,*' said Iasus. '*Maintain position and vector of advance.*'

The answer came back so quickly, Sirras wondered whether Iasus had understood him. He tried again. 'Theoretical: any strategy whose result is the faster extermination of the enemy must be explored. Practical: a drive to the canyon would accomplish just that. We would lure the orks to us, while forcing them back over the cliffs.'

'*I am aware of the potential in what you propose,*' Iasus replied. '*My answer is the same. Request denied.*'

Sirras spoke through gritted teeth. '"*Dogmatic adherence to initial strategies is the surest warranty of defeat,*"' he said, quoting the *Prologomena*.

'*My refusal is not the product of rigidity, captain. It is the result of analysis. Practical – your manoeuvre would open up a gap in our lines. Theoretical – the opportunity you would provide the orks is of more potential value to them than any possible benefit to us. You have your orders.*' Iasus cut the channel.

Sirras clenched his fists. Nicandrus kept his attention carefully focused on the screens.

'Alert me of any other such geological features,' Sirras said, keeping what face he could.

'As you wish, captain,' Nicandrus answered.

Sirras climbed back out of the hatch. With a snarl of anger, he jumped from *Eknomos* at a charging ork. The brute wore thick plates of crude armour. It carried an axe whose blade was half the size of Sirras. He ducked under the swing and stabbed upwards with his lightning claws. The blades sliced through the armour as easily as the flesh. Sirras brought them all the way up through the greenskin's jaw and out the top of its skull. Sirras withdrew the claws and the ork fell. Behind it came more. Infinitely more, Sirras thought.

Hierax, you should be here, he thought. *And you should be leading Nemesis.*

Where the plain ended, the ground rose steeply. When the First Chapter reached it, the flood of orks coming from this sector of the cordillera had dwindled. Guilliman could see large steady flows still heading to the battle to the north and south. The spearhead had taken its toll, though. Here, at least, the orks could no longer attempt to sweep away the Ultramarines in a wave of brute force.

There was a way up the slope for the tanks. The orbital scans of the mountains had revealed the telltale switchback patterns of roads at regular intervals leading up from the plain. Now he could see the state of those roads. They were badly pitted and cracked. Rock falls had caused further damage. Guilliman moved the Vindicators to the lead, and as the column made its way up, the tanks' siege blades saw heavy use. The blades and cannons were needed to clear rubble to such a degree, the climb was tantamount to a siege.

From midway down the column, Gage voxed, *'How long have the orks been on Thoas? They seem to have been very busy.'*

'No more than a century or two,' Guilliman said. The figure was approximate, based on incomplete records pieced together from the other reclaimed worlds. There was enough consensus in the fragments to gather some sense of the systems' histories during the Age of Strife. 'This damage is not all the doing of orks,' he said. He doubted any significant amount had been caused by the greenskins. He saw the scorch marks and scrapes caused by the passage of the xenos army. They were clearly recent. The collapses and piles of debris were older. He saw the workings of erosion. The road had not been maintained for a long time. He frowned. This was not what he had expected to find.

The final switchback led to a wide approach to the main gates of the ruins. The advancing Legion had forced the remaining orks back. They rallied now before huge doors. The entrance to the ruins was a hundred feet high and sixty wide. The doors had a dark sheen. Though they were blackened, they showed none of the wear of the road. Guilliman suspected they were an alloy of adamantium and iron. They were engraved with huge runes in a language Guilliman did not know.

The doorway was built into the wall of a structure as monumental as its entrance. The decaying pyramid emerged from the mountainside as if it were being extruded by the rock. Seen closer, the stone of its construction, though it had come from the mountains, had been machined to the point of being unrecognisable. The stone was smooth, deep black, and formed into gigantic slabs. The structure rose to a position just below the mountain peaks. It was angular, suggestive of being a half-buried octagon. The walls of each terraced level leaned outwards. Their angle, combined with the vertical thrust of the pyramid, made the ruin seem to loom over the two armies, perpetually toppling, yet unyielding.

At regular intervals along the face of the mountain chain were more pyramids, all half emerging from the rock, all with their battered roads leading to their entrances. Narrow spires of the same black rock emerged here and there from the peaks themselves. Between the pyramids were clusters of huge pillars and collapsed structures that could have been temples or palaces. Where the structures had fallen, they seemed to be merging back into the mountainsides. The most visible aspects of the ruins were the gigantic pyramids. In the regularity of their spacing, Guilliman thought they resembled battlement towers, with the mountains themselves serving as the ramparts.

The orks howled their challenge and rushed down the incline of the approach.

'Bolter fire only,' Guilliman ordered. 'We will preserve the ruins.'

The tanks held back, and Guilliman charged forwards with the legionaries of the First Chapter. Their stream of mass-reactive shells shredded the front lines of the orks. When the two forces met, the greenskins had already lost half their number. They still fought hard. For the first time in this campaign, it seemed to Guilliman the orks were struggling to keep a possession. The ruins were theirs, and there was outrage in their snarls as they tried to push the Ultramarines back down the mountains.

Guilliman held the trigger down on the *Arbitrator*. He sent death before him, and when he reached the bleeding horde, he struck with another weapon of death. *Incandor* flashed in his hand, severing limbs and throats with every gesture. He used his own body like a battering ram, slamming into brutes who cried out with pained surprise when it was they, and not their prey, who were sent flying backwards in the collision. He trampled over bones and skulls. He was a machine of efficient slaughter. He wasted no energy or gestures on any one foe. He butchered with grim conviction, but not with pleasure. The xenos had no place on Thoas, and it offended him that they should try to claim a human relic as their own. But he was not Angron. Guilliman killed with brutal efficiency. He took satisfaction in victory, and in the validation of strategy.

When he and his sons trampled the orks out of existence, they were extinguishing animalistic war with reasoned war. The brutish gave way to thought. This was the inevitable movement across the galaxy. His father brought enlightenment, and the old savageries had no choice but to fall away.

The clash before the gate was brief. The Ultramarines out-numbered and outgunned the orks. When the smell of fyceline cleared, the enemy was a ruin of blood and shattered corpses covering the ground before the doorway.

Guilliman advanced to the doors. 'Marius,' he voxed, 'will you join me?'

Flanked by his Invictarii honour guard, he studied the runes on the doors while he waited for the Chapter Master Primus.

'Can you read them?' Gage asked when he arrived.

'No. The language is definitely human, but pre-Gothic.'

'How can you tell?'

Guilliman pointed to a rune a third of the way up the left-hand door. 'The parallel lines on that one, and the linked curve. There is a family resemblance there to the runic inscriptions we found on Aletho Two. These are older.'

'You were correct, then. Human inhabitation of Thoas has a very long history.'

'Yes...'

'You sound uncertain.' And Gage sounded alarmed.

Guilliman smiled. 'Not to be at this moment would be intellectually dishonest.' He gestured at the ruins visible along the curve of the mountainside. To the north and south, the columns of the other Chapters were fighting their way up the slopes to their designated pyramids. 'The damage to this civilisation strikes me as being very old too.'

'Then the orks have been here longer than we supposed?'

'Perhaps. Let us see what waits for us inside.'

The doors opened easily for their size. Guilliman had chains attached to each door, which were then pulled by Rhinos. Metal ground against stone, and the way opened to the Legion. Guilliman walked in first with Gage at his side. Behind them marched the massed companies of the First Chapter. The heavy armour came next. The entrance was wide enough for the tanks. While the Predators entered the pyramid, Guilliman ordered a line of Vindicators to remain at the entrance, facing outwards as the first line of defence against an attempt by the confused mass of orks at the base of the mountains to reclaim the ruins.

Beyond the doorway was a chamber so vast the air felt hollow. The roof of the pyramid had fallen in, revealing the grey of the cordillera's perpetual dawn. Helmet torches and vehicle lights shone their beams over the walls. There had once been many levels inside the structure, but they were gone now. Scraps of metal marked where they had been, level with each of the exterior terraces of the pyramid. The flagstones of the ground floor were deep in greenskin refuse. Heaps of metal wreckage combined with organic filth. Guilliman could see twisted, jagged and torn fragments that might have once been stairs or decking. On the walls were murals. They were so faded it was impossible to tell what, if anything, they once represented. On the lower levels, the orks had defaced the interior with their own crude artwork – red and black grotesques in the shape of horned, snarling faces.

'So this is where the orks scavenged their material,' Gage said.

'So it would appear.' Guilliman looked up the height of the pyramid. If all the levels had had metal decking, the orks would have found untold thousands of tonnes to use. Guilliman stared at one of the greenskin scrawlings. 'Do you notice anything about the walls?' he said.

Gage turned around, scanning the space. 'The orks have only defaced the lower regions,' he said.

'Exactly.' There was some ork handiwork visible as high as the first level or so, but it was scattered. By far the majority of the totemic faces howled on the ground floor. 'Why would that be?'

'They were too occupied tearing down the interior?'

'Perhaps.' Guilliman didn't like the explanation. It was too simple. It made no allowance for the animalistic enthusiasms of the greenskins. They were not mindless. They were not servitors. He walked to the nearest wall. He examined the overlapping ork faces and the original art beneath. Some of the ork art was quite recent. Some he could well believe was over a century old. Their colours had faded, but nothing to the degree of the murals. All of the greenskin efforts were still clear. 'What if the levels had already collapsed?' said Guilliman. 'The wreckage would have been piled quite high initially.' He pointed up. 'The greenskins could have indulged in some of their art while salvaging the top of the heaps first.'

'Those faces higher up do look more faded,' Gage said.

Guilliman nodded. 'Older,' he said. 'And the murals are older yet. Much older.' He gazed at the hole in the pyramid's roof, hundreds of yards above him. If he had the time to examine the edges of that gap, would he find evidence that the orks had somehow caused that damage? He thought not.

'If the floors had already collapsed…' Gage began.

'Yes. Theoretical – this civilisation had already fallen when the orks arrived.' He ran his gauntlet over the wall. 'There is a gap in time here,' he said. 'These murals have been fading for much longer than they have been defaced by the orks.'

'What do you think happened?' said Gage.

'Too early to speculate.' He pressed his lips together. 'Cultures do not need an external enemy to fail. They are born, they age, they lose their coherence, and they collapse. There is a remembrancer from the Age of Terra, a Willem Yaitus. My Father showed me one of the fragments of his works that have survived. He wrote of the cycles of civilisations, and of their inevitable end. "*Things fall apart, the centre cannot hold,*" he said. That is the tragedy of human history until now, Marius. That is the cycle from which my Father is saving us.'

Guilliman sighed, gazing at work that had become its own forgotten memory. He grieved for what had been lost. He had come to Thoas not expecting anything beyond the task of necessary extermination. He had held his hopes in check when the ruins had been discovered. He had told himself there would be nothing to salvage beyond restoring another piece of human history. He had taken for granted there would be no living humans to find. To hope for something different at the heart of a greenskin empire would have been madness.

You were hoping for something, though, weren't you? he thought. *Yes. Yes, I was.*

He had hoped for signs of a heroic end. The civilisation that had built these ruins had been capable of grand gestures. Their fall to the orks would not have been without a vast struggle.

But they did not fall to the orks.

He already knew what he would find as the Legion made its way deeper into the ruins. There would be evidence of decay, of a culture growing tired and losing its way. Fatigue, erosion, retreat from the heights once reached, and the collapse. There would be no glory there. He did not like to think of the orks bringing energy to the world, yet that is what must have happened. The greenskins had arrived to find an empty shell, and they had turned it to their own violent but vital ends.

He shook the melancholy away. The reclamation was still useful. Thoas would become part of Ultramar. It would live again, with the energy of light and reason. And its history would emerge from the night into which it had fallen.

There was value in that.

'What do you think the purpose of this structure was?' Gage asked.

'You sound like you have some thoughts in that regard.'

'Theoretical – a military command centre.'

'The metal decking,' Guilliman said.

'Yes. Very functional, but not suited to a hab zone.'

'Your theoretical implies a similar function for the other pyramids.'

'It does.'

'By extension, this entire region of the mountain range is a single fortress.'

'Particularly if the pyramids are connected.'

'A fortress entails defence,' Guilliman mused. 'Defence against what?'

'I can't speculate.'

Neither could Guilliman. Gage's supposition made sense, but it raised many questions.

'We will find the answers,' Guilliman said. 'Once we have consolidated our position.'

He voxed Habron. 'Are the orks moving our way yet?'

'*Some,*' the Techmarine said. '*Not in significant numbers. The current preparations will be enough to keep them out. There are battles to the south, but the larger portion of the horde is north of us.*'

'Your evaluation of the enemy's state?'

'*Still a viable force. Without knowing their precise numbers before we began…*'

'Feel free to extrapolate.'

'*Our strategy appears to have borne fruit. The initial push by the First Chapter created a central focus for the horde, resulting in the formation of a core. The second wave destroyed that core. The ork force has been reduced.*'

'You're not going to guess by how much, are you?'

'*The attempt would be irresponsible.*'

'Agreed.' Habron was right to be cautious, but the evidence of the success of the initial blow was clear. Guilliman turned back to Gage. 'We move north. We will learn the extent of the ruins, and reinforce the other Chapters. We have the high ground now. The orks must fight upwards from the plains, and their wave will break against our positions.'

There were wide, arched passageways leading out of the pyramid at three levels, equally spaced on its great height, heading north and south. The upper passages were beyond reach, but the ones on the ground floor were immense, clearly designed to accommodate the mass movement of vehicles and crowds.

Troops, Guilliman thought. Gage was right. The ruins had the marks of a gigantic military redoubt.

And still the question: *Against whom?*

He led the way, and the First Chapter began its march into the dark, bringing light, seeking illumination. From deep in the ruins, the howls of orks echoed against stone.

The 22nd Chapter took the entrance to the northernmost pyramid three hours after the first one fell to the Ultramarines. Iasus' companies were the furthest north, and they were the last to enter the ruins. Iasus was conscious of that fact. He heard the reports over the command network of the vox as he fought his way up the mountainside. He heard the other Chapters storm the ruins, take possession, and begin consolidation. He was not troubled about being the last. What troubled him was Sirras' reaction. He knew the captain disagreed with the order not to make a push towards the canyon. It was not until the companies of the 22nd had breached the pyramid that he realised the depths of Sirras' discontent.

'*We are losing the initiative, Chapter Master,*' the captain voxed.

'Explain your analysis,' Iasus said, more out of necessity than interest. The final push to the lower doors had been bloody. The orks had mounted a ferocious defence, bursting from the interior of the ruins in a huge wave. Their mass alone had been enough to push two Land Raiders and a Rhino off the side of the approach. They had fallen, rolling end over end, to a crushed, explosive end on the plain a thousand yards below. Now Iasus stood in the centre of the pyramid's enormous ground-floor chamber, his armour drenched in ork blood. His nostrils and lungs filled with the clammy foulness of the brutes with every breath. Around him, the troops of the 221st Company established an impassable wall of ceramite at the entrance while reconnaissance squads prepared to venture through the north entrance into the further ruins.

The losses across the companies were high, and these legionaries hardly looked on him as a brother, even those who had been born on Macragge. Sirras was edging close to insubordination, and Iasus no longer had the patience to tolerate his resentment.

'The rest of the horde is being sealed out of the ruins by the other Chapters. The orks have seen that we are last, our position as yet unsecured. They are shifting their efforts to our destruction.'

'Then we are well-positioned to destroy them when they arrive,' Iasus said.

He was standing beside his command Rhino *Praxis*. He ended the conversation with Sirras and banged on the side. Techmarine Loxias slid the door back. 'What can you tell me?'

'The greenskins coming up behind us have slowed. Theoretical – they are remaining out of range of our defensive guns until reinforcements arrive.'

'How long will that be?'

Loxias turned and examined his screens. 'Longer than I would have predicted. The horde as a whole appears to be slowing at the foot of the mountains.'

'Are you sure?'

'I have confirmed my readings and analysis with the auspex systems of the other companies and Chapters.'

Iasus frowned. He distrusted anything that smacked of good news when it came to the orks. The only truly positive development would be their extinction.

'Speculation?' he asked. He entered through the Rhino's side hatch to get a better look at the auspex.

'None that satisfies, Chapter Master,' said Loxias. 'The behaviour is uncharacteristic.'

Iasus tapped a pict screen. 'The horde looks smaller than it did earlier.'

'It is occupying a smaller area,' Loxias confirmed.

'Because of their losses?'

'Perhaps. And perhaps a greater concentration.' The Techmarine did not sound happy with his reasoning.

'You don't think so.'

'Contraction of area and decrease in speed are both accounted for by the premise of greater density.'

'But…?'

'The tactical benefit is limited. How many more orks could attack us at one time?'

'You're assigning them the ability to strategise. These are orks, brother. They could simply be confused, too. If they are coming after us, we present a multiplicity of targets… and a multiplicity of points to defend,' Iasus muttered. The reports from the other pyramids painted rather different pictures from what the 22nd had encountered. All the other structures had suffered massive internal damage. All their upper floors had collapsed, and the metal decking had been scavenged by the orks. This most northern of the pyramids was closer to being intact, inside and out. The approach to the southern face split up into four ramps, each rising more steeply than the last in order to reach the upper entrances. The interior floors were constructed of stone instead of metal. The floors were many feet thick, easily able to support the infantry and armour. Each level was empty, a huge, echoing chamber void of equipment and purpose except for the stink and debris of greenskin life. The walls were covered in vague, faded murals and ork obscenities. Ramps wide enough for two tanks to take abreast came down on the eastern side of the chamber.

'You have reported what we found to the primarch?' Iasus asked.

'I have been speaking to my counterpart in the *Flame of Illyrium*,' Loxias corrected. 'Lord Guilliman emphasises the need to preserve this pyramid.'

Iasus had come to the same conclusion himself. The ruins

were the human history the Ultramarines would take back from the orks. If there was anything to learn, this pyramid offered the greatest opportunity.

'There is something else,' Loxias said. He changed a setting on the pict screens. A schema of the pyramid appeared. It glowed a bright red. 'Radiation levels in this structure are much higher than those recorded by the other Chapters.'

'How bad is it?'

'Prolonged exposure would be fatal to mortals.'

Which meant it should still be within the tolerance of the genhanced bodies of the Legiones Astartes, further shielded by their power armour. Even so, the anomaly was significant.

'Can you identify the source?'

'No. At present it is too widespread.'

'Is this a bombing after-effect?'

'There is no visible damage.' Loxias changed the display to show the radiation reading across the mountain chain. 'There is radiation everywhere in the ruins,' he said, showing Iasus the readings. 'It is consistent with the effects of an ancient bombing over the other structures. The degree of radiation is correct, assuming a conflict at least a thousand years ago, and likely much earlier.'

'But this pyramid is undamaged,' Iasus said.

'Yet the radiation level is much higher.'

'Yes.'

What do you do with this information? Iasus wondered. *You do nothing in this moment,* he told himself.

'Excuse me, Chapter Master,' Loxias said with a notable change in tone. 'The primarch will address the entire Legion.'

Iasus straightened as Guilliman's voice reverberated out of his vox-bead. '*Ultramarines,*' he said, '*we shaped the battlefield on the plain. Now we will do so again. We forced coherence on the foe and shattered its centre. Now we will shape the war once more.*' The voice was rich in strength and certainty. Guilliman spoke from knowledge, experience and study. There was no hubris in what he said. His words were measured, his assertions chosen with care and all the more inarguable. Iasus listened to the primarch speak, and heard the sound of inevitable victory. *'Theoretical - the strongpoint controls the narrative of the war, forcing the foe to react within a narrowed range of possibilities. Practical – we will take and hold the ruins. Purge the ruins of the greenskins. They will attack, and the wave will break for the final time.'*

When Guilliman had finished speaking, Iasus addressed the 22nd. 'Brothers,' he said, 'we will have the honour of being the point on which the wave will break. Make our defences strong. The orks will believe they are laying siege to us. In reality, they will be making themselves vulnerable to our terminal advance.' He thought for a moment, then stepped out of the Rhino and opened the private channel to Sirras. 'Is everything clear, captain?' he said, speaking coldly.

'Perfectly, Chapter Master.'

There was no more warmth in the reply.

'As mazes go, at least it's spacious,' Rizon said. The Scout of the 223rd looked up and down the intersection, faced with a choice of empty darkness.

Tarchus grunted in agreement. The sergeant pictured the tunnels crowded. The image was disturbing. It emphasised the wonder of the civilisation's total disappearance. Millions must have worked here, and with great purpose. The military nature of the ruins was more than clear now.

Beyond the pyramid, the tunnels became a network, and then a warren, each branch leading to more. Tarchus could foresee the tunnels leading off for hundreds of miles into the cordillera. Smaller tunnels, some still wide enough for a single vehicle, ran off the main ones at irregular intervals. Beside the largest intersections, shafts that could swallow a Vindicator gaped. There were vertical grooves in the shafts. *Perhaps the remnants of a form of grav lift,* Tarchus thought. The mountains were so hollowed out that their exteriors now seemed insubstantial.

Many of the routes were blocked by rockfall, and Tarchus' squad had to double back or choose alternative routes so many times that it became impossible to plan a systematic reconnaissance of the ruins. There were more squads in the tunnels, and the 223rd was only in the network that led off the third level of the pyramid.

Here and there, the collapses were extensive enough to open the tunnel to the sky. The cold wind of Thoas moaned through the tunnels like a spectre of loss. Some of the gaps were very wide and circular. *Bomb damage,* Tarchus thought, *and not recent, either.* The edges of the craters were rounded from erosion. Scree had accumulated beyond the gaps, blown in by the wind.

Everywhere, there were marks of the orks having made the ruins their base. But the damage they had caused simply by existing in this space was visibly recent compared to the craters and cave-ins. The complex had died long before the orks had arrived.

Scout Fierelus came back from having explored the next hundred yards of the eastward passage. 'More of the same,' he said. 'And still more branching.'

Tarchus nodded. It was time to report to the captain once more. He contacted Sirras on the vox. 'Our status is the same,' he said. 'No sign of the enemy yet, and the region we are meant to control appears larger the more we see of it.'

'*Can it be held?*' Sirras asked.

'Not in the sense of an occupation. This network is large enough to hold millions.'

'*Your recommendation is to hold the pyramids.*'

'It is. Let the enemy come to us. The orks will, anyway. They don't skulk. We won't have to go looking for them.'

'Very well,' Sirras said after a minute. *'Make your way back to–'*

A huge, echoing, discordant howling cut Sirras off. It came from every direction, growing louder as it rode its own echoes. The greenskins were here and they were close.

'Contacts!' Tarchus yelled.

'None!' Rizon said. 'They're out of auspex range.'

The amplification of the sound was making the orks seem closer than they were, Tarchus realised.

'To all Scouts of the Twenty-second Chapter,' he voxed. 'Does anyone have readings on the enemy?'

His answer was a confusion of voices, all asking the same question. Then Zarachas of the 221st shouted, *'We have them! Coming up fast two hundred yards north-north-east of the pyramid!'*

'Scouts,' Iasus broke in. *'Withdraw. Return to strongpoints.'*

'We're pulling back,' Tarchus told his squad. He led the way back down the tunnel at a run. He held his bolter ready. 'Watch the auspex,' he told Rizon. He gave the Scout the coordinates Zarachas had reported.

'That's between us and the pyramid,' Rizon said.

'Yes, it is.' They had worked their way over a thousand yards north-east into the ruined network.

Tarchus listed to Zarachas' voice as he ran. The Scout updated the ork movements every few seconds. They were closing fast.

'They must be coming up the shafts,' Fierelus said.

'Then why hasn't there been line-of-sight contact yet?' Rizon asked.

Zarachas' reports ceased. His vox-cast dissolved into a blizzard of static, shouts, and gunfire. Then it cut off.

A moment later, Rizon said, 'I have them.'

'Where?' Tarchus demanded. *How?* he thought. The squad was still hundreds of yards from the reported position. Unless the orks weren't coming straight up. He blinked his visor lenses to prey sight, but there was still nothing.

'Everywhere,' Rizon said. The Scout spoke with grim resolution. He knew and accepted what was about to happen.

The echoes were deafening. The walls themselves were howling, as if the tunnels had become bestial maws. On the vox, the reports from the other squads were a fragmented cascade. Auspex contacts turned into running battles within moments. There was no way to gauge the size or direction of the horde.

Rizon was right, Tarchus realised. *They are everywhere*.

The orks attacked when the Scouts reached the next junction. They poured out of the side tunnels. They surged from every minor break in the main passageway walls. As if a dam had burst, the green tide filled the tunnels.

Everywhere.

Tarchus and his Scouts opened fire, shooting ahead and behind. They still headed for the pyramid, because those were their orders, and there was no action that made sense any longer except the fulfilment of duty to the end. They ran down a tunnel wide and high enough for a flight of Thunderhawks. From one side to the other, it was filled with orks. Tarchus ran towards the wave. A single squad charged thousands of greenskins. Behind, Tarchus heard the thunder of many iron-soled boots. He fired, and he saw orks fall. He fired, and he was trying to kill an ocean.

Solid shells from ork guns thudded against his armour. They chipped the ceramite. A lucky shot took out his right lens. A crossfire hail between the two hordes cut down dozens of orks. It was so thick the impacts felt like power fists slamming into Tarchus' front and back. The Scouts didn't have the armour to withstand so concentrated a barrage. They went down, their bodies punched through with dozens of impacts. Rizon was last. He staggered on at Tarchus' side, his left arm broken, armour and carapace shattered, the holes in his torso too large for the scabbing agency of the Larraman's Organ. He was bleeding out as he fought.

'Purpose…' Rizon gasped.

'Fulfilled,' Tarchus told him, hammering shells into the onrushing orks. He dropped more.

We have served, he told himself. *The orks have come for us first. We have bought the Chapter time to prepare.* He shouted warnings into the vox. He gave his position.

Rizon was silent, staggering on, still shooting.

'Beware the walls!' Tarchus voxed. 'The orks know of other shafts. They have the run–'

A gigantic ork put on a burst of speed and stormed ahead of the rest of the horde. It was a monster, twice Tarchus' height, its face a snarling mass of scar tissue surrounding savage tusks. It swung a huge axe as it closed with Tarchus. Bullets hit him from behind. He staggered forwards, running into the edge of the blade. It smashed through his gorget and severed his throat. He could not speak. He could not breathe. Blood filled his lungs. He raised his bolter, holding down the trigger, stitching the ork through torso and head.

The orks at the rear stopped firing. They caught up. A cleaver came down through Rizon's skull. Tarchus turned to avenge the Scout. A beast with a metal fist punched him in the chest. His armour held, but the blow pushed him back. He stumbled into the weapons of the other orks. The greenskins hacked at him with cleavers and axes as heavy as they were crude. The orks hit him with blows that would have cut a mortal in half. He sank beneath them. He was still firing, and he heard the cries of wounded monsters.

There were other shouts too. They were tinny, small, and in his ear. They came from Sirras, shouting the names of the 223rd's Scout sergeants. None were responding.

Tarchus tried, but he was choking on his blood. His arms were tired, moving far too slowly, while the orks attacked him with the speed and power of uncontained, explosive life.

He was still struggling to speak as the darkness came down over his eyes. He hoped his captain had the time he needed to prepare.

Silence fell before the dark. The orks' jaws were wide, but no sound came from them.

The blades cut through the gaps in his armour. The weapons rose and fell. He looked at them with detachment. It was as if they were no longer striking his body.

Is this enough? he wondered, but could not ask.

He sank to the ground, drowning in the green tide.

Conflicting tactical needs must be resolved through the rigorous application of the theoretical. The theoretical is the method by which the relative value of the competing priorities can be determined. This determination is critical. To choose the wrong tactical need is to hand weapons to the enemy. The error can easily compound to the point that this single choice can lead to defeat regardless of the foe's tactics. Indeed, the opponent may not have any strategy at all. War is a force unto itself, and though it is shaped by the decisions, correct or disastrous, of the combatants, it is not controlled by either faction. At best its force can be directed, and the power to do so is useless if it is not applied correctly. Thus, not only is the theoretical the necessary precondition to victory, so is its absolute rigour. The decision made in the conscious absence of the theoretical is the guarantor of self-inflicted doom.

– Guilliman,
On the Practical Necessity of Theoretical, 22.5.lv

FIVE

INFESTATION • PRESERVATION • APOSTASY

The mural made Guilliman pause. This was before the word came from the 22nd. This was in the final seconds during which the war on Thoas followed the narrative he had established.

In the pain of the years ahead, he did not often think back to this moment. It would be superseded by far worse memories, and far worse agony, far worse narratives. But even in that period of cursed innocence between Thoas and Calth, when so much of what he believed was burning and he did not know it, he did not like to think of this moment. He willed his mind to slide over the memory when he considered Thoas. There was much he would choose to put aside about the world. He would tell himself the memories and the thoughts they engendered were unprofitable. That they were irrelevant or worse. Their suppression was an active good.

These were the things he would tell himself. And later, when the galaxy burned, and he was confronted by his blindness, there would be the fresh pain to come from this campaign. He would be reminded of all that he had not seen, and of all that he had chosen not to see. He would see the patterns and the

repetitions in his blindness, and the terrible alloy of grief and
rage would be forged anew.

Guilliman and the companies he had selected to accompany
him were deep into the ruins. They were making their way
northwards. The route was circuitous, angling through multiple blocked intersections. They were taking the largest tunnels,
wide enough for the full deployment of heavy armour. The
passages could have been grand avenues. Stretches hundreds
of yards long were open to the sky where the high roofs had
fallen in. There, as in the pyramid, Guilliman saw murals faded
to vague blurs of colour.

Here, though, now, in the last moments of the narrative he
had decreed, he and his sons were in an untouched section of
the tunnels. The passage led across a colossal domed chamber.
A mustering zone, Guilliman surmised. The orks had pillaged it
of metal too, though there were more traces of the higher plat-
forms. Their size suggested they had been landing pads. The
floor was thick with debris, and the stench was eye-watering.
Orks had made a home of this chamber. A century of deface-
ment covered the lower walls. Higher up, the original murals
were intact. They were dark from the decades of smoke from
dirty fires, but the wind did not reach this far in. The artwork
had weathered time better than in any of the other regions the
Ultramarines had crossed.

The lights of the vehicles shone on the mural. Guilliman
paused at the sight, Gage at his side. The companies waited
for him. The vehicle engines idled, their guttural rumbles filling the dimness of the dome with echoes. Guilliman looked
up, studying the mural. It was martial in theme. That was no
surprise. Commanders a hundred feet tall struck heroic poses.
Their forces were faded hints behind them.

'Those shapes look familiar,' Gage said, pointing to rough
silhouettes.

'Land Raiders,' Guilliman said. 'Then they had Standard Template Constructs.' His gaze returned to the commanders. They held his attention. They made him uneasy. *Why?* he wondered. *Analyse the details.* Piece by piece, there was nothing he could point to and state was objectively wrong. The cut of the uniforms, the shape of the caps, the stern visages – each detail spoke to the authority of these men and women and celebrated their prowess.

Perhaps the answer was in the obscured portions of the mural, in the murky colours that had lost all form, but still gestured towards meaning.

'These soldiers are lacking,' Gage said.

'Agreed,' said Guilliman, and he came closer to finding what displeased him. 'I have no sense that they are fighting in the name of anything.'

'They do seem to be *against* the name of something.'

'Yes. And only that.'

The moment of contemplation was a long one, though it lasted mere seconds. And when Guilliman's dislike of the murals crystallised, the vox burst into life.

The ork counter-attack had begun. They were everywhere along the length of the ruins, and the 22nd Chapter was taking the worst blows.

The wave of greenskins appeared at the edge of the tanks' illumination. They rounded the curve of the tunnel and charged towards the ground-floor access to the pyramid. They howled with victorious rage. At the huge doorway, Iasus stood between Land Raiders. He waited a few seconds more, for the orks to be scores deep. They filled the width of the tunnel completely. If any of the smaller greenskins wound up on the sides, they were crushed against the tunnel walls by the bulk and momentum of their larger cousins.

This is not a choke point, Iasus thought. *The tunnel is far too wide. We might as well be fighting in the plain again.* 'Fire at will,' he said.

Las-beams seared the enemy column. They incinerated multiple orks at a stroke. Heads and torsos became ash. Heavy bolters chewed up the forward ranks. The leading mass of orks vanished in an explosion of blood and torn flesh.

A few blasts punched all the way to the far wall. Rock vibrated. The tunnel hummed, then shook. In the lights of the tanks, the air turned grey with a snowfall of dust and rock chips. Cracks ran down its length. The tremors increased with every second of artillery fire.

'All companies!' Iasus voxed. 'Cease heavy fire. Infantry only! The structural integrity of the ruins is compromised!' The pyramid's solidity was an illusion, he realised. Whatever had damaged the other structures and punched craters through the tunnel roofs had punished this portion of the ruins too. It was a monument waiting to collapse.

The Land Raiders of the 221st fell silent. The orks raged forwards over the annihilated bodies of their kin. The tremors continued. Iasus could feel the pounding rhythm of ongoing shelling from one of the upper levels. It resonated through ceilings and walls, even into the rock under his boots.

'Cease fire! Cease fire!' he shouted into the vox.

The rhythm ceased. The tremors eased. But the dust still fell, in the tunnel and in the pyramid's chamber.

The orks were two-thirds of the way down the tunnel. Large-bore but crude bullets shrieked into the Ultramarines line. Thousands of brutal axes and sword blades were raised, the bloodlust a tangible musk.

'Brothers of the 221st!' Iasus shouted. He raised his power sword. The dust created a bright nimbus around its blue light. 'Forwards with me! Courage and honour!'

They were his brothers. Many of them might not think so.

Perhaps none of them did. But he was their Chapter Master, and when he called, they answered. A battering ram of blue and gold ceramite charged out of the pyramid to meet the orks. The barrage of bolter shells was orders of magnitude beyond the power of the swarm of ork bullets. They inflicted almost as much damage as the Land Raider guns. Scores of greenskins died. For a moment, the ork wave seemed to stop where it was, the brutes dying as quickly as they ran forwards.

The illusion was short-lived. The wave was too huge, too ferocious. It closed with the Ultramarines, its thousands of voices united in a single, shattering roar.

In the final seconds before impact, the leading edge of the Ultramarines phalanx narrowed to a point. On either side, the ranks further back poured on the bolter fire. The spear point drove into the orks with power sword and chainblade.

The momentum of the two forces was such that Iasus had a sense of accelerating as he cut and shot his way into the green tide. Orks thundered past him, ignoring him in favour of the legionaries ahead of them. He butchered the orks before him, his movements an efficient, murderous refrain. In these initial seconds, they came at him, and he at them, too fast for them to defend against his blows. He swung his power sword through a neck, decapitating the greenskin with a single swipe. The head flew off to the left. The stump geysered blood. Iasus fired his bolt pistol through the crimson, drilling massive holes through the skull of the next ork before the body of the first had fallen. He brought his sword back the other way and into the neck of a third ork as the other bodies crumpled. Three enemies dead in two steps.

He ran on, a lightning scythe, slashing and shooting, slashing and shooting, moving deeper and deeper into the enemy lines. Behind him, the legionaries of the 221st took down the greenskins, each brother striking with his preferred weapons and techniques, the individual approaches forming a unified killing machine.

For as long as half a minute, the Ultramarines advance stopped the wave cold, a wedge driving deep into its core. Half a minute when the attack to defend the pyramid seemed on the verge of becoming a true advance.

That illusion lasted much longer than the first one. Then it died too. The orks kept coming. The river of brute strength was unending. Giants waded through their smaller kin. One reached for Iasus. He pumped three shells into its chest. He destroyed its armour fashioned from scavenged metal plates. Fist-sized wounds opened in its torso. The ork snarled in agony but didn't slow. The impact of the shells was enough to spoil the aim of its own blow, and it hit Iasus with the side of its axe blade, hard enough to snap the weapon in half.

Iasus heard cracks on the left side of his armour as he flew against the rampaging orks on his right. He crashed to the ground. He was trampled. Bodies fell on him, holding him in place. He roared and fired upwards, pulling the trigger so quickly that the explosions of the shells blew apart the corpses and hurled his attackers back, bleeding and dying. He rose just as the giant ork reached him again. The warlord shouted in its barbaric tongue and grabbed his shoulders with both hands. It lifted him high, squeezing as if it would crush him to pulp. As it raised him, he plunged his power blade forwards. The ork gutted itself. It stopped for a second, staring at him in disbelief and anger, holding him with its arms outstretched. Then it let go, and he plunged back into the cauldron.

There were more huge greenskins arriving, slower than the others but much more dangerous. Harder to kill, too. And still the orks kept coming. Their fury and energy grew with every second of violence.

The Ultramarines advance slowed, then stopped. Now the orks

were coming faster than they could be killed. They blunted the wedge of the 221st.

'Make a wall,' Iasus voxed the company. 'Let none pass!'

The wedge grew wider, stretching from wall to wall. The lines of the Ultramarines were deep. The orks had nearly a thousand legionaries to fight through if they wished to reclaim the pyramid.

They mean to, Iasus thought.

On the heels of that thought came another, even less welcome. The orks were not fighting to take back the ruins. The greenskins engaged in war for its own sake. They would attack until they or the Ultramarines were no more. And wasn't that why the Legion had come to Thoas? To exterminate the orks?

The ruins had changed that. Guilliman had ordered they be saved and held. So now Iasus fought to preserve as well as to destroy. Envy of the orks flashed through his hearts. They fought without restriction, and by instinct alone. They had a wild freedom in their way of war.

He dismissed the envy in the same moment. He ran his sword through the eye of another brute, and in doing so he hurled the unworthy emotion away. There was no value in the ork way of being. There was no purpose. There was no meaning.

But there was power and relentless strength in their hunger and the greenskin multitude. The 22nd truly was fighting a tide. With every kill, Iasus was trying to swim against a savage current, and no matter how many orks he shot and slashed, his blade and pistol could no more stop the relentless flow than they could kill the sea. The orks roared and charged and fought and died and fought and charged, endlessly. The 22nd could not stop the greenskins from reaching the pyramid. The strongpoint would fall.

We don't need to stop them.

The thought was a revelation and it was liberation. He almost

laughed as he sidestepped the axe swings of two orks, took a
step back and drilled them with bolt-shells. *Theoretical: preservation of the ruins is contingent on the completion of the initial goal of
extermination. Practical: do not fight to hold ground. Fight to destroy.*

What he had envied was the Ultramarines' to take. There was
no need for a strongpoint. The ruins would be theirs when the
last ork lay dead.

'Our fight is not defensive,' he voxed the Chapter. 'Seek the
opportunities of the moment. Annihilation is our watchword!
Let them come and fall on your blades. Brothers, there are no
reserves. We are all on the front lines!' The shift in tactics was
a nuance, but its importance was more than psychological. The
only thing to defend would be a brother's flank and back. The
Ultramarines formed into tighter, smaller, more mobile formations, unbreakable stones in the midst of the ork torrent.

The battle roar that greeted his orders gave him new energy
and hope. He hurled himself at the xenos, slashing and shooting. In the heaving tide of the horde, it was difficult to gauge
direction. No matter. Every direction was forwards. The ground
he covered was irrelevant. A step back was not a retreat. What
mattered was each ork that fell. Every kill was the true way
forwards.

A few yards to his right he saw two legionaries go down. The
muzzles of their bolters glowed red from the rate of fire. The
orks came at them so fast that their disintegrating corpses hit
them with the heavy weight of dead meat. There were multiple blows, and for a moment the bodies were shields for the
greenskins behind. Orks slammed into the legionaries and overwhelmed them with numbers. Iasus tried to cut through the foe
to reach them. It was too late. The bolters kept shooting for a
few moments more, but cleavers and axes struck arms and legs
and heads and torsos at once. Shrieking chainblades ground
through the seams of armour. Iasus was only two steps away

from the mob that had obscured the legionaries when the floor was awash with a new flow of blood. It was not the stinking, obscene blood of orks. It was heroic blood.

Iasus severed the spine of one of the attackers. He sprayed bolt-shells in an arc before him. He brought retribution.

The orks died, but the horde did not care.

Theoretical: each of our losses is a true step back.

There was no countering practical.

His strategy was sound, but in the end, it would hinge on numbers. Each Ultramarine was irreplaceable. Every ork that died gave way to twenty more. The shift in tactics had bought time. He had hoped it would be enough time to stem the tide at last.

It was not.

'Courage and honour!' Iasus shouted again. The words were the truth he lived as he fought. They were the ultimate worth of victory.

He did not know if they would be enough.

Guilliman led a forced march through the tunnels, heading north at speed, cursing every cave-in and detour that slowed the advance. The reports from the other Chapters were coming in fast. They flowed through Habron, who updated Guilliman as the situation changed. And it was changing too quickly.

'All pyramids are currently under attack on two fronts,' Habron said. *'By siege and infiltration.'*

'The scale of the interior battles are something more than infiltration,' Guilliman corrected.

'Acknowledged, primarch. The…' Habron paused. Guilliman heard him mutter quietly and dispassionately to himself as more data poured in. *'The primary enemy forces are indeed inside the ruins,'* Habron continued.

'What is the state of the external attacks?'

'In all but one case, those orks are being held outside the pyramids.'

Good, Guilliman thought. If the orks had linked up with each other, that would be a sign of the battle going badly for the Ultramarines contingent at that location, and the signal for things to grow much worse.

'The orks at our initial location are being contained outside. There have been no attacks from the inside as yet.'

More good news. Guilliman had left a much smaller force to hold that pyramid than was inside the others.

'The pattern we noted from the start is remaining consistent. The orks are in greater concentrations in the northern sectors of the ruins.'

'Questions that need answers,' Guilliman said. 'Why that pattern? And where are they coming from?' The streams of orks down the mountainsides had greatly diminished in the final stages of the Ultramarines' drive through the plain. He had thought the supply exhausted. It was not like the orks to hold a reserve.

'The strength of the interior attacks is much greater than available data would have indicated.'

The avenues of attack also troubled Guilliman. The orks had staged what amounted to surprise attacks. The warnings of their approach were too short, their numbers too great. He looked at both sides of the tunnel his phalanx was marching through. The passage was so wide, the walls were barely visible, shrouded in deep gloom. He eyed the smaller passages as the lights of the tanks flashed over them. Inside those side tunnels, he knew, were still smaller tunnels. The Scouts from all Chapters had reported finding them, the minor byways of the endlessly proliferating labyrinth of the ruins. *Theoretical: smaller shafts exist within these tunnels as well.* The orks had had over a century to learn all the routes through the labyrinth. The idea of the brutes having the strategic foresight to use unexpected hidden routes struck him as flawed, yet it was the best analysis he could make with the information he had.

Practical: anticipate attacks in this region even when they seem unlikely.

The unanticipated was already under way everywhere else.

He opened the command channel on the vox once more. 'Ultramarines, hear me. We are coming. You will be reinforced. Hold against the orks, and we will destroy them together. I am advancing north. We will exterminate the enemy one step at a time. At every stage, our victories will free up more troops to assist. Our retaliations will grow more terrible. Legionaries of the Twenty-second, your battle is the most heroic. Hold fast. Your brothers from all Chapters will soon be punishing the greenskins at your sides. Together, we have already claimed this fortress. Together, we will purge it.'

He stopped talking. He sniffed. His lips pulled back in anger.

'*Contacts,*' Habron warned.

'I know,' Guilliman said. In his rage, his boots struck the floor with greater force as he marched. They sent chips of stone flying. 'Marius,' he voxed to Gage. The Chapter Master Primus had returned to his position midway down the column. 'We do not stop. We do not slow. No. Matter. What.'

'*Understood.*'

They came, then. The orks burst from the dark. Along a third of the length of the phalanx, they roared out of the side passages. Howling tributaries flowed into the main tunnel, forming a wave on each side of the Ultramarines. The waves came in, surging in the face of bolter fire so intense that the muzzle flashes filled the tunnel with blinding, strobing, killing silver day. They came from the front too. The huge passage extended for hundreds of yards, curving gently to the west. Guilliman heard the mob and smelled it before it came into sight. He ran faster. He was fury now. These thoughtless creatures were anathema to everything he held to be true about war. They were an offence against everything the conduct of battle should be.

Now they had dared to disrupt the narrative he had brought to Thoas. They had done enough damage. He charged the orks as if their refusal of any rational form of war were a personal affront.

Guilliman opened fire with the *Arbitrator*. He and the Invictarii struck first. Their charge was faster. It was more furious.

It was more dangerous.

The tunnel erupted. The orks died and died and died.

Still they came, their animal revel undaunted.

In the strategium of the *Cavascor*, Hierax watched the tacticarium screens. He listened to the litany of reports coming from the bridge below the command pulpit. Servitors recited lists of shifting coordinates in their flat voices. The dead recitations suggested nothing of the meaning they carried, their news of shifting battles and growing losses. The augur and vox officers delivered their updates in clipped, precise tones. Hierax read their tension in their posture, subtly changing from unbending to rigid.

The news from the 22nd had him swinging between frustration and rage. In the strategium, he filtered the vox feed so he heard only the command channels of the Chapter. Several times, he was on the verge of speaking. He held back each time, waiting until his picture of the battle was clearer, keeping his voice out of the clutter of communications. He would speak when he was of use.

The situation the rivers of data formed was grave. He could see how the primarch was countering the orks. Guilliman was sweeping north. The other Chapters were holding their own. Reinforcements would surely tip the balance against the greenskins. The strategy would create cascading reinforcements, the victory of each position providing the means to guarantee the triumph of the next, until the combined might of the Legion struck the largest concentration of orks attacking the 22nd.

Already the gunships were pounding the exterior positions of the orks outside the northernmost pyramid.

'Not enough,' Hierax muttered. The orks outside were a distraction.

There were three levels of fighting in the pyramid. The Chapter was divided, and the orks were not. From the orders shouted by the Chapter Master and the captains, Hierax tracked the rapid shifts in the conflict. The disposition of the forces was fluid.

Theoretical: the primarch will not arrive in time.

Practical: the Destroyers can.

I can end this.

Hierax broke in to the combat channel. He would be heard by all the senior officers. 'Chapter Master,' he said. 'Requesting authorisation for the drop pod insertion of the Second Destroyers. We can be at your position within minutes. Our weapons–'

'Authorisation denied,' Iasus said. He grunted as if something had hit him. The other voices faded out momentarily as close bolt pistol fire drowned out the rest of the feed.

'Our brothers need us,' Hierax said.

The channel was still open, the exchange still being heard by the other captains. Hierax was on the edge of insubordination. The other captains said nothing. Bursts of explosions and chainblade growling marked their individual struggles. The sounds vanished. Iasus had changed the communication to a private one.

'Our orders are to preserve the ruins,' said the Chapter Master. *'Yours are to await the command to deploy. Not to initiate it.'* He cut off the vox.

Sirras drove his chainsword into the chest of the warlord. The ork was not much taller than the others around it, but it was wider, a tank of flesh and bone. It carried hammers in each hand, and swung them forwards to batter Sirras' armour. The blows were tremendous, and the ork kept striking as the chainsword whined through muscle and ribcage. Blood spurted. For several seconds, Sirras was blinded by a deluge of crimson. The hammers hit him again and again. Another ork attacked him from behind. He was drowning in red and green.

The blood flowed off his helmet and he shoved his chainsword all the way through the ork. Its arms fell limp. Its torso split with a tearing of muscle and fell backwards. Sirras whipped the chainsword around and into the flank of the ork behind him. The smaller brute shrieked as the teeth of the blade chewed its flesh apart. Sirras cut the ork down one-handed. He fired his bolt pistol to the right, three shots taking off the upper half of the skull of a greenskin rushing at him with a sword as long as a man's arm. He was surrounded by bodies. They were hemming him in. The orks kept coming, and his movements were more and more restricted. A green wall was trying to bury him alive.

It was trying to bury the entire company. Sirras had followed the strategy commanded by Iasus. He had led the charge against the orks. He had known from the start it would not succeed. The orks were simply too numerous. With the support of the heavy armour, the greenskins would have been hurled back. Progress in the extermination would have been made. With the tanks idle except for heavy bolter turrets, the orks surged forwards, trampling over their dead. The charge of the 223rd Company was bogged down before the first junction. The great xenos wave battered the Ultramarines. It overwhelmed individual brothers. It sapped all forward momentum. The horde flowed around the legionaries. No matter how many they killed, more still came. They rampaged through any gap in the lines. Every Ultramarine who fell opened the way to the orks. The flood found the cracks in the dam, and the orks forced the 223rd back and back.

Sirras shouted in frustration. He turned full circle, sawing through limbs and sending shells through skulls. There was no retreat, Iasus had voxed as he changed tactics. Every dead enemy was an advance. Perhaps that was true for the Chapter Master. Maybe the orks weren't pressing as hard two levels below. Up here, things were different. Up here, Sirras killed with as much fury and speed as he ever had in his decades of service to the Legion, and still he was going backwards. Even if he was standing still, he was losing ground.

The losses were mounting. Iasus kept urging all the companies of the Chapter to keep on the offensive. *We've lost the offensive*, Sirras thought. The 223rd was fighting for its survival. The density of the ork horde in the tunnel was like a moving wall. Even if all the orks in that mass were dead, it would have pushed the Ultramarines back.

'Close formations!' Sirras urged. 'Shoulder to shoulder! We are each other's shields!'

The order was unnecessary. The company was already contracting. He spoke to be present in the ears of the legionaries who, like him, had become isolated in the flood, their nearest brothers having been brought down.

There was no forwards. There was only the green tide, and perhaps the hope of retrenchment. Sirras turned and killed, turned and fought. He cut an ork in half vertically. The body fell apart, and between it he saw a fractured squad forming, a small island in the midst of the storm. He lunged in that direction, sawing and shooting through bodies. Axes and cleavers chopped into his armour. Orks shot him at point-blank range, injuring themselves with the ricochets. The bullet impacts began to take their toll. Damage runes flashed amber and red in his helm lenses. Servo-motors whined. There was a drag in his left leg, a microsecond delay between his impulse to move it and the armour's response.

He compensated. He fought harder. He blocked a chainaxe,

its motor spewing smoke. Sword and axe shrieked against each other. He shot at the orks hacking at his right flank. Another slammed a cleaver into his left. The chainaxe leaned more heavily against his sword. He ignored the blows on his sides and brought his pistol forwards. He fired a burst into the ork and into its weapon. The greenskin dropped and the axe exploded, raining burning promethium over the combatants. Liquid flame sloughed off Sirras' armour. It coated the faces of his nearest attackers. They struck wildly through their blindness, howling anger and pain. He dispatched them with furious contempt.

He was that much closer to the squad.

He snarled as he butchered his way forwards. He saw other lone warriors, like him, fighting their way towards the group. At the back of his mind, he was aware that his combat technique had become less precise, more savage. He raged in frustration at the constriction of space that made the elegance of his combat skills useless. He raged at the enemy, and at the currents of war that had turned to run in the orks' favour.

He raged too at his Chapter Master. Hierax had requested deployment. He had seen the need. Iasus had shut his answer off from the captains. *Why bother?* Sirras wondered. *If you don't want us to hear what you have to say, then we can guess all too easily what you said.*

There was no longer any sense in the tactics that had governed the campaign until now. There could be no preservation of this region of the ruins. The true aim of the campaign – annihilation – must be the touchstone.

This was obvious beyond any need for analysis.

He burned with the need to strike back hard, to carve victory from the enemy's hide with all the force of his frustration and hatred.

Massive force against massive force.

He gave voice to his rage.

'Land Raiders,' Sirras said. 'Heavy weapons reauthorised. Targets as before. Fire at will.'

The tanks had not changed position. The enemy was everywhere. Their hatch gunners were firing heavy bolters in a three hundred and sixty degree arc. They had killed hundreds of orks, and prevented them from storming the roofs of the tanks. They were surrounded by heaps of sundered bodies and brass shells, yet they had managed to clear no space, or to ease the pressure of the howling, slavering horde. They were at the entrance to the tunnel, forming a line Sirras had intended as an obstacle, but which had been no more than rocks in a foaming river.

Now they would be more.

Six pairs of twin-linked lascannons fired as one. The tunnel filled with molten light. Hundreds of orks perished in a single moment. Radiant heat blasted back through the pyramid, so intense it blistered skin. The sound was beyond searing, a shriek molecular and gigantic. As the scream faded, the chatter of the heavy bolters became clear again. The guns were pounding the corridor wave once more, tearing apart more of the stunned greenskins as the lascannons powered up.

The Land Raiders fired a second time.

The air in the pyramid smelled of fire. The heat was cumulative. So much energy into so many bodies, the organic mass of the orks making the vast space claustrophobically small. Weapons designed for the open battlefield incinerated the interior wall.

The Land Raiders fired a third time.

'Captain Sirras,' Iasus voxed. *'What are you doing? Cease fire! Cease fire!'*

Sirras silenced him. *I am winning this war,* he thought.

A fourth barrage.

A fifth.

The rock of the tunnels began to glow. The heat was turning

lethal. On the other side of the tanks, in the pyramid's chamber, Sirras saw some of the smaller orks stagger, their flesh smouldering. The pressure of the horde diminished.

Sirras joined up with the squad. Their coordinated fire annihilated the orks before them, and for the first time in hours there was space to move, and to turn the art of Ultramarines warfare against the greenskins. The ork losses grew.

The lascannons fired, and fired, and fired. The shriek of energy and the skull-crushing boom of the blast wave became the call and response of a choir of perfect destruction. The song resonated to the beat of Sirras' hearts. It seemed his anger had stepped beyond him, become a terrible entity, and was striking out at the world of the ruins. He could even hear the pounding of its fists, and the cracking of the ruin's bones.

The sound of those blows grew louder yet, and Sirras realised what he heard was real. Something even greater than the star-born fury of the lascannons had come. The sound was huge, deep, terminal.

Sirras looked up. The glow of the rock in the tunnel had spread like veins over the stone of the pyramid. Flames and muzzle flares created more illumination. Sirras saw the cracks rush up the walls to meet at the pyramid's apex. A hail of rock fragments began. Larger and larger pieces fell to the floor of the upper level.

He saw the entire structure begin to twist like a tree in the wind. The stones beneath his feet shook. They began to move in different directions.

The pyramid groaned. It wailed like a thing alive, a thing that had woken to the world only to breathe its last.

The darkness of millions of tonnes hurled itself upon him.

The clear-eyed understanding of war must perforce include the understanding of the disaster. The disaster is the reality that the will to victory chooses to dismiss, and therefore courts. This is not to say the disaster must be anticipated. Yet it must be expected. Even in the most rigorously reasoned campaign, mistakes will occur. Beyond the control of the commander are the events of chance. The unforeseen can never be extinguished from war. Disaster waits in the error, in chance and in the unforeseen. The skilful leader will seek to stave disaster off, but over a sufficiently long time period, the disaster becomes inevitable. It is not regarded as such, however. Fatalism is as injurious to battlefield success as näiveté. The battle must be fought as if the disaster is impossible until the disaster is real. How it is countered is the true test.

– Guilliman, *Treatise on the Disaster*, 23.17.v

SIX

DISASTER • NOTHING • REMAINS

There was another junction ahead. Orks appeared in the left and right branches, running to join the battle. They were welcome to their demise, Guilliman thought. But either direction was wrong. To the north was another collapse. This was a major one. A large portion of the mountain roof had fallen through, crushing tunnels, leaving a sloping pile of debris that rose through open air. Guilliman evaluated the rise as he ran forwards, barely seeing the greenskins he slew. The largest boulders were scattered. Vehicles could get around them. The slope itself was not precipitous.

'We climb,' he ordered.

The Chapter rolled over the greenskins. The orks attacked in the hundreds, but they were not enough to blunt the advance. They charged into their doom as if they were energised by victories elsewhere, a spirit of brutal triumph infusing every ork on Thoas.

Guilliman ran up the slope at the same pace as in the corridor. The air was clear, free of the greenskin stench. The collapse created a path that ran between two peaks. The Ultramarines followed it, moving north at good speed now. The ridge took them higher than any of the pyramids.

'Too much to hope we can travel the rest of the way above ground,' Gage voxed.

'Likely,' Guilliman agreed. They were still climbing. He could not see beyond the pass. He made no assumptions. If the other side of the pass was an impassable gorge, so be it. He would have the tanks blast openings back into the tunnels if necessary, though he did not think it would be. When he looked down the mountain slope to his left, he could see the signs of other collapses, the echoes of explosions from centuries past. 'We go as far and as fast as we can,' he said. 'This is who we are.'

'*"The unplanned campaign is as futile as the inability to improvise",'* Gage quoted.

'I can't decide if I'm that memorable or you're that obsequious.'

'Neither,' said Gage. *'It's the truth that's memorable.'*

Guilliman smiled. 'Exactly,' he said. 'You do understand, then. Leadership finds its value in truth, not the other way around. This is why no leader is irreplaceable.'

Gage did not reply. No doubt he did not appreciate having his words come back to him in the form of that lesson. Guilliman took his silence as a sign of understanding. He did not protest, and that was all Guilliman asked of him.

The pass was narrow, as if the peaks had been cleft by an immense axe. The speed of the column slowed as its width contracted. The tanks had to follow each other in single file. Between the vertical faces of the peaks, the penumbra of the sky became a strip of grey. As he pounded along scree and stretches of bare stone, Guilliman wondered again about the culture he had found in this narrow habitable zone of Thoas. The tunnels could well extend east, indefinitely, through the entire cordillera. Perhaps there were true arcologies to be found. The civilisation that had built the pyramids and the cave network had clearly been capable of constructing something on the order of Calth's underworld.

He was struck, though, by the total absence of above-ground structures further east. The ones in this section were minor in comparison to what lay inside the mountains. Even so, they were monumental; easily detectable by the orbital augur scans. To the east, further into the dawn, there would be regions of endless gentle light and the most moderate temperatures on the planet.

Yet there was nothing at the surface there. If the tunnels went on, that deep, would they have the same aspect as here, on the western edge of the cordillera? His initial evaluation of the pyramids as being part of a fortress seemed to have been correct. Everything in the tunnels and larger chambers was martial. He had seen nothing that suggested a use beyond the rapid transport of armies and the housing and maintenance of huge forces.

Again, in defence of what? Where were the cultural artefacts of this civilisation? Where was *anything* except its empty shell of military defence?

And yet again, against whom? The signs of ruinous war were everywhere, but no sign of the enemy that must have, in the end, triumphed over the Thoasians. There was only the emptiness, the hollow echo of a world now occupied by the opportunistic orks.

The pass curved to the right, then opened up again. The Ultramarines emerged from between the peaks. The ridge sloped downwards, rather more steeply than it had risen to the south. A spire rose from the ground at the exit of the pass. It was a hundred and fifty feet tall. It leaned precipitously with the slope. The top was jagged. Stones from the demolished upper portion littered the slope. Its former use was obvious: from this vantage point, Guilliman had a clear perspective of every pyramid to the north. He could see the size of the horde laying siege to each position. The way forwards looked promising. The ridge was unbroken and its grade manageable all the way down to the nearest pyramid.

Guilliman saw the means to make concrete his new narrative of the war, one he would impose on the hubris of the orks. The necessary revisions were becoming clear to him when Habron voxed him.

'*Tank fire in the northernmost pyramid,*' Habron said. '*Against Chapter Master Iasus' orders.*'

'Who?'

'*Captain Sirras. Iasus is trying to get him to stop. The pyramid's structural integrity is weak. Sirras has disobeyed–*'

The groan cut Habron off. It cried out along the length of the mountain rage, bouncing off rock faces, gaining power and momentum as the upper half of the pyramid began to lean. It made a half-twist, a monument bowing to its unseen master. The groan turned into a thunderous roar as the pyramid collapsed. Its shape disappeared. It fell in on itself and the mountainside. The mountains seemed to shake as the stones smashed down on the orks and the slope below. The boom of the impact grew louder, becoming a greater, cracking thunder.

The mountains really were shaking.

'Sirras,' Guilliman muttered. 'What have you done?'

The peak above the pyramid slumped. The movement was so vast it was deceptively slow. Tens of millions of tonnes of rock broke away. The mountain's face sloughed off. It slid down, a gigantic sweep of total destruction. The roar was the sound of the sky shattering. The silhouette of the mountain vanished in the billow of dust. The cloud raced across the mountain chain, swallowing the war. In less than a minute it reached Guilliman's position. Thoas disappeared into black limbo. The thunder would not stop.

Guilliman stood in a choking void. He saw nothing. He heard nothing except the world's cry of pain. The war was gone. All narrative was gone. Everything had fallen into an abyss. There was no direction in which to march. There were no decisions possible.

In the void, he was seized by a psychic vertigo. Everything melted away. There was no theoretical to construct. No practical to enact.

There was nothing.

Nothing.

The vertigo was too strong. A catastrophe was unfolding, but his reaction went further than was warranted. Something deep within him, something he could not identify, was reacting to the dust-blindness. *Look!* it cried. *Look!* it demanded, roiling with impotent, desperate frustration. *You do not see!*

No, he did not. There was nothing to see.

Nothing.

Except time. That still existed in this void. It was data, something that could be measured and had implications.

Guilliman counted the seconds. He marked each minute, each painful period that his column was immobilised, unable to move forwards and bring reinforcements to the Chapters below. The seconds elapsed, the roar of the rockslide faded, and the limbo began to give way. The dust remained thick, but he could hear again the sound of war. In the positions closer to Guilliman, further from the 22nd Chapter's disaster, the struggles inside the tunnel network would not have been affected. The war was ongoing. The passing of each second changed the configuration of what Guilliman would encounter. The cost to his legionaries grew. The means he would have to employ to alter the outcome became more and more important. He did not know what actions he would take. He could not know. Yet he felt the scale alter, and he prepared.

Theoretical: the force necessary to counter lost time increases exponentially with respect to the time.

Practical: overwhelming force, employed from the start, reduces the degree of necessary adjustment.

The seconds and the minutes passed. The dust began to settle. Guilliman waited. The downward slope became visible.

'*We can move forwards once more,*' said Gage.

'No,' Guilliman answered. 'Not until we see the extent of the disaster. Knowledge is more important than speed at this juncture.'

He waited, the seconds and the minutes marching by. The initial stages of the disaster created enough interference to wreak havoc with the vox. Habron re-established contact now with the Chapter Masters and captains, except for Iasus. From within the fallen pyramid, all was silence. Guilliman listened to the updates. The new picture of the war began to form even as the cloud still covered everything but the upper peaks of the chain. Contact was sporadic with Empion and Banzor, commanding the Ninth and 16th Chapters in the strongpoint closest to Iasus' position. That was cause for concern. It was also information Guilliman could use. So when the dust finally cleared enough to reveal all, he was prepared for what he saw.

The northern pyramid had disappeared completely, its location buried under the slide. The face of the mountain was exposed, revealing a network of tunnels as dense as a hive. Orks boiled out of the tunnels like an insect swarm. The horde flowed over the devastated landscape, making for the next base. That pyramid, though still standing, had lost a large portion of its northern face. On instinct, the orks were doing precisely what Guilliman had attempted. The thousands upon thousands of warriors would be added to the force already fighting the Ninth and 16th. The wave would grow larger with each position overtaken, washing back towards the south as it drowned the Ultramarines.

My strategy reversed, Guilliman thought. He noted the irony. It did not amuse him.

Theoretical: the orks must be countered with an equivalently larger force.

There was no way for him to reach the interior of that pyramid in time.

Practical: pull the Ninth and 16th back to the next pyramid south. Concede ground in order to mount a more powerful counter-attack.

He voxed Empion and Banzor. It took several attempts before the Chapter Masters could speak. He explained what needed to be done. 'Can you withdraw?' he asked.

'I cannot,' Banzor replied. *'The pressure from the interior is pushing us north.'* His signal faded, fuzzed into static, then came back. He spoke through a filter of gunfire. *'We are immobilised between the two primary hordes. And damage to the structure is limiting our movements even further.'*

'Empion?' Guilliman asked.

'Doubtful. The collapses have been extensive here as well. Withdrawal might be possible, but…'

'At great cost to the Sixteenth,' Guilliman finished.

'Our formation is defensive,' Banzor said. *'The orks have us surrounded. Empion is relieving some pressure on our southern flank. Even with that, we are barely holding the orks back.'*

'Understood. Both Chapters will continue to fight as your situation dictates. You will not be alone long. Courage and honour.'

He gazed at the landscape before him. Disaster had altered it. Disaster had also created opportunity. He would use Sirras' foolishness to reach his goal much sooner than would have been possible until now. Guilliman switched channels to speak to Gage and Habron. 'Bring in the gunships,' he told the Techmarine. 'All of them. I want an airlift of our forces to the north side of that pyramid.'

'How deep in the tunnels is Banzor?' Gage asked.

'It doesn't matter,' Guilliman said. 'We will fight the orks on the slope. We will destroy them there, and open the way for Banzor.'

'Gunships re-routed,' Habron reported.

'Good. Artillery, commence a bombardment on that slope. Disrupt ork movements until we arrive.'

A minute later the Whirlwind and Basilisk tanks unleashed their anger. As the first of the Thunderhawks arrived, the rubble of the slide erupted with explosions. The missiles created a storm of flame and flying rock. The shells of the earthshaker cannons cratered the wounded land, turning boulders into powder. Orks vanished in every blast. They were everywhere on the land, and they died everywhere. The movement of the horde slowed. It was not enough. It was firing shells into a moving stream. But the disruption was real.

The Thunderhawk *Masali Spear* landed on the slope before Guilliman. Its engines whined, eager to fly again as the assault ramp slammed to the ground. Guilliman charged up the ramp, leading the Invictarii. 'We drop between the artillery and the open wall of the pyramid,' Guilliman ordered on the command vox.

Masali Spear rose to make room for the next gunship. It circled the landing zone, joined by one Thunderhawk after another. Guilliman slid back the side door of the troop hold. He stood in the centre of the opening, immovable in the shrieking wind, visible to every Ultramarine who turned his eyes skywards. He spoke to the Legion.

'We are confronted with the result of error,' he said. 'Action without reason is self-defeating. See this moment, my sons. Learn from it. We respond to the irrational with reason, with analysis, and we march to victory. The orks are unreason. They cannot hope to win. They have no defence against our most powerful weapon. Reason. It is in your blood. It is our heritage from my Father. Be who we truly are. Let every shot and blow be governed by reason. Know yourselves and the impulse behind every action.'

He paused as yet more gunships rose to join the squadron. The chorus of the engines was tremendous. The Thunderhawks formed a great storm, a cyclone of adamantium hulls and ablative ceramite armour. They circled, machines of terrible destruction transporting gods of annihilating war.

'Look at us!' Guilliman shouted. 'We are my Father's judgement! We are the devastation of reasoned war!' As *Masali Spear* flew along the southern arc of its circular flight, he pointed to the north. 'Now!' he said. 'Now we show the orks the power they must fear!'

As if given impulse by his arm, the Thunderhawks flew north, to where reason hammered the ground to dust.

The icons in his lenses were nonsense. They flashed white through crimson. Iasus blinked them off and on several times. He managed to cycle the photolenses through to low light, and he could see again.

The floor of the pyramid had collapsed into a lower tunnel complex. The walls had come down between them. The organisation of the network was destroyed. There was no way to tell the difference between a chamber and fused tunnels. He was surrounded by the chaos of broken stone. Slabs leaned in a jumble of diagonals or were heaped high upon each other, forbidding passage. The ceiling was ten feet high at most. In many places it was much lower. Rubble pressed in from above, heavy with the promise of further crushing falls.

Iasus wasn't sure if he had been unconscious. His memory was jagged and full of gaps from the moment the pyramid caved in on itself. There had been weight and death and falling, and a colossal hammer of darkness. Now the gloom was lit by guttering flames. There were no more explosions. He smelled promethium. A few yards to his right was the wreckage of a Land Raider. It had saved his life. It had been destroyed by the rock fall, but it had held the rubble far enough from the ground to spare him.

'Captains of the Twenty-second Chapter,' he voxed. 'Respond.'
There was no answer.
He switched to an open channel, and called to any survivors

of the 22nd. One by one at first, then in clusters, his legionaries answered.

So few? he thought.

'Form up on me,' Iasus said. He made his way forwards to a fallen monolith. There was just enough room between its peak and the ceiling for him to stand upright. It was the closest he could see to high ground. Ork blood oozed from beneath it. Iasus could hear snarls coming from some distance in the gloom. In his vicinity, he saw nothing apart from smashed greenskin bodies. The only survivors here had been wearing power armour.

Even so, he wondered how many were left.

'Loxias,' Iasus voxed.

'*Chapter Master.*' The Techmarine's voice was suffused with pain.

'Where are you?'

'*I am unable to determine that. In any event, the question is moot. I am still in* Praxis.'

'It survived?'

'*It did not.*'

'I see.'

'*I am pinned, Chapter Master. The lower half of my body is not viable. I believe the Rhino is buried. I may be able to restore some systems' functionality. I am working on that now.*'

Shadows moved through the maze of rubble towards Iasus. The survivors of the 221st Company gathered at his location. 'Communications?' Iasus asked Loxias. The vox signals were erratic. He had tried calling to the other Chapters and heard nothing. He suspected proximity was the only thing permitting contact with the remnants of the 221st.

'*I believe so.*'

'Is there anything from Captain Sirras or the 223rd?' Iasus had tried several times already.

'*The auspex is working,*' Loxias said. '*No life signs detected above this region. The destruction appears to have been total.*'

'Thank you, Loxias. If you can restore communications with the rest of the Legion…'

'*You will be the first to know.*'

Iasus scanned the legionaries around him. There were fewer than a hundred. Their squads were fragmentary. Iasus saw only two squads that appeared to have their full complement of warriors. 'Brothers,' he said. 'We are reduced in numbers, but not in effectiveness. We adapt and do what we must. That is our culture. That is our strength.'

'What are your orders, Chapter Master?' asked a legionary in the armour of a tactical veteran.

Iasus searched his memory for the Ultramarine's name. 'Burrus,' he said, 'we shall make our way out and join the other Chapters.'

Burrus nodded. 'Out where?'

Iasus looked up. Dust trickled down from the ceiling of packed, broken stone. 'Theoretical,' he said. 'If all life is extinguished above, the collapse has likely been total. We are buried beneath millions of tonnes of stone. Practical – we find a way to go even further down. When we find intact portions of the network, we head south.'

'We are with you, Chapter Master,' Burrus said. He rapped his fist against his chestplate. So did the others.

Burrus was from Terra, Iasus recalled. He had performed his duty well and followed orders without question, but his resentment of Iasus had been clear from the start. He was not a legionary who had aspirations of command, that much Iasus could tell. But he was one who had strong opinions about the fitness of his leaders. In Iasus' few interactions with him, he had been almost completely silent. Never outright insubordinate, yet not hiding his unhappiness about the outsider Chapter Master.

There was no resentment now. The question had been an honest one, and Burrus was satisfied with the answer.

Iasus turned around on the slab. In every direction was a mass of heavy shadows and jumbled gloom. Every direction was equally unpromising. There was no obvious descent.

Theoretical, he thought. *Given how extensive the network is, and our position in the ruins of multiple junctions and chambers, to head off in any one direction will inevitably result in the arrival at a shaft or more intact tunnel.*

Practical: choose a path and advance constantly.

He made his choice. 'This way,' he said, pointing east. Down that way lay their brothers, no matter how far they had to go.

He was right. Ten minutes later, after climbing over and around rubble, they reached a shaft. It was a small one, barely wide enough for a legionary wearing armour to negotiate. Iasus led the way, climbing down.

There were snarls below.

They were growing louder.

Look upon every enemy action as a revelation. Every attack and manoeuvre discloses motive, means and intent. Should the foe's strike be successful, unless it results in your defeat, it is now the most detailed knowledge in your possession of the enemy's tactics, weapons and strength. Remember that the enemy is also learning from you. It is the consciousness of this accumulation of knowledge that becomes the critical point. The commander whose understanding is swiftest, and most finely developed, will turn the enemy's strength into a weakness, and march to victory.

– Guilliman,
For a Hermeneutics of Strategy, 96.34.iii

SEVEN

SALVATION • DEPLOYMENT • SURVIVAL

The gunships flew over the battlefield once before landing their troops. They pounded the slope with Thunderhawk cannons and cluster bomb payloads. Guilliman watched from the side hatch. A huge cloud of flame and dust rose up, expanding fireballs sending out a storm of debris. For hundreds of yards, the approach to the pyramid became a new hell of destruction. To the west, the artillery bombardment continued. The movement of the orks was disrupted. Guilliman saw them scatter in confusion, change direction, collide. The flow of the green tide became turbulent. Thousands of bodies littered the broken landscape. It was a good start.

It was only a start. The orks covered the slope. They were still closing with the pyramid. From this side, the true extent of the damage was visible. Most of the west side of the structure had fallen, leaving a huge mound of rubble leading up to a gap hundreds of feet wide. Orks were leaping from boulder to boulder as they climbed the rubble before leaping into the pyramid. Even with the interdicting fire of the Thunderhawks, the orks were flooding inside.

'*The pilots want to bombard the entrance,*' Gage voxed.

139

'Permission denied,' Guilliman said. 'Banzor and Empion are lucky the pyramid is standing at all. We will do nothing to bring it down on their heads.'

'*Understood.*'

'One more strafing pass,' Guilliman ordered the gunship pilots. 'Then prepare to land us. Ultramarines, make ready to jump. We strike on the downslope run.'

Aboard *Masali Spear* was an armoury reserved for Guilliman's use. From the ornate, gleaming brass chest he took the *Hand of Dominion*. He donned the power gauntlet. He flexed his fingers. The fist of crimson and blue crackled. Energy coruscated around its form as if hungry to be unleashed. The choice of weapon was a reasoned one. It was the right weapon for the type of landscape and the type of war he was about to wage. But it was an emotional choice too, a fact he had forced himself to confront and reflect upon before he gave himself license to indulge in it. He had had enough of the orks. Most of all, he had had enough of how their savage, unthinking way of fighting was reversing his gains, and doing so by engaging in a way of war that was a mocking mirror image of his strategies. The orks would not win. They would be crushed. He would crush them with his own hands.

The gunships finished their uphill run. Smoke and billowing dust rose in their wake. They turned, *Masali Spear* in the lead, and roared back down, flying within a few yards of the ground. Their sponson-mounted heavy bolters hammered the ground ahead, clearing the path of the orks that had survived the bombs and the cannons. The horde continued to arrive from the north, but there was a gap now.

Masali Spear slowed midway through the dark, choking cloud. Dust whirled in violent eddies as the gunship blasted its hull nozzles down and forwards, approaching a hover. Guilliman leapt from the side door. His sons followed. In a few seconds, thirty Ultramarines deployed onto the rubble. *Masali Spear's* engines surged and it flew up, angling towards the north. Behind it, other gunships were already disembarking their warriors. In less than a minute, the full complement of the First Chapter's infantry was on the ground. The gunships resumed their bombardment, moving north and east, beyond the artillery barrage, to hit the orks as they emerged from the exposed hive of tunnels.

The wind of Thoas blew away the smoke. The orks appeared, the tide frothing over the rubble to the north. The leading brutes howled a challenge at the sight of the wall of Ultramarines. The greenskins behind picked up the roar. It spread. In an instant, the shattered slope resonated with savagery's call to war. It was louder than the bombardment. It was a long, throat-tearing ululation, the voice of a species that lived for the joy of war and would revel in that joy until its last warrior died.

And that, Guilliman thought, *is why we will exterminate all of these brutes.*

He raised the *Hand of Dominion,* and he answered the orks with a roar of his own. He wanted them to understand what they were dealing with. His sons joined him. The roar of the Ultramarines was a deep, powerful bellow. It was the sound of nobility enraged. It was the sound of savagery's doom.

Guilliman charged, the Invictarii at his side. On his right, further up the slope, Gage led another forward wedge of Terminators. The rest of the legionaries followed a moment behind. The Ultramarines came for the orks not as a wave, but as a wall, a human siege blade with battering rams to the fore.

The perception of the orks as a single, solid mass dissolved as Guilliman drew closer. The terrain prevented anything like the density of fighting in the plain and in the tunnels. The slope was steep. The footing was treacherous. Smashed, jagged rocks varied in size from loose, rolling scree to slabs the size of gunships. Guilliman barrelled straight at a loose cluster of huge brutes. They had drawn together as they saw him, each monster wanting to claim his head as their prize. He opened fire with the *Arbitrator*, spreading his fire between the five giants. Armour shattered. One ork fell when a shell slammed though its eye and its brain exploded out of the back of its skull. The others were wounded to a blind rage. Streaming blood, they hurled themselves at Guilliman, vaulting over boulders. They were beyond reckless.

Guilliman met them with controlled, strategic wrath. The first ork reached Guilliman a second before the others. It was twice his height, a being of uncontrolled, uncontrollable fury. Guilliman hit the warlord with the *Hand of Dominion*. The gauntlet slammed into the ork's ribcage with a flash of azure energy. It punched through the greenskin's body with the force of a meteor. It incinerated flesh and muscle. It pulverised bone. Guilliman angled his strike downwards, and his blow went straight through the ork. His arm disappeared into the beast's disintegrating torso. His fist came out the other end, through the ork's spine, and struck the boulder behind. The light was dazzling in the sombre dusk of the mountains. The shock wave blew up the boulder and the ork. It knocked the nearest greenskin flat. The other staggered, blood fountaining from its nose and ears. Its howl was now one of pain. It clutched its head. Guilliman took it down with a quick burst of the *Arbitrator*.

The last tried to rise. Guilliman slammed the *Hand of Dominion* down again. Rock and ork were vaporised in the blow. The earth shook as the impact rippled outwards. Boulders shifted. Debris rolled down the slope. A precarious heap of granite collapsed, starting a new slide, knocking more orks off their feet, crushing their howls into silence as the rock gathered momentum down the slope.

Their helmet crests waving in the eternal wind, the Invictarii incinerated greenskins with plasma pistol blasts. They ran through and dismembered any who managed to get close with power swords. The blades hummed and flashed. They were works of beauty and elegance. Guilliman appreciated art, and he understood its worth in the battlefield. It was the signifier of greatness, of the superiority of the warrior honoured to wield the object whose worth exceeded its ability to kill. But more than art, more than beauty, Guilliman valued precision. The power swords were the right weapons for the right warriors. In the hands of the Invictarii, they were the art of war crystallised into a simple, murderous form.

Orks died. With plasma bursts and power gauntlet concussion waves, their deaths were brilliant flashes in the twilight and the cracking toll of a stony bell. The flares were bait. The currents in the greenskin tide shifted. Brutes who had been rushing to the promise of battle in the pyramid now charged towards the closer, brighter fight. The bellows of their dying comrades were a summons rather than a warning.

Guilliman saw the shift, saw the growing number of enemies heading towards him, and he was satisfied. *Theoretical: the orks will turn from besieging Banzor if a more immediate target presents itself. Practical: hit them hard, and be as visible as possible.*

Now they came. Guilliman and Gage's wedge formations hit them first. Guilliman repeated the principle of the assault on the plains, forcing the orks to come together in an effort to stop his advance, and tearing out the heart of the hordes. Behind came the long, deep line of legionaries, their steady stream of bolter shells, rockets and flamers meeting the orks that ran on.

The howls of the orks became more and more outraged. The horde came for the First Chapter.

'Movement behind us,' Gage voxed. *'Some of them are pulling out of the pyramid to fight.'*

'Good,' said Guilliman.

'We'll be surrounded soon.'

'Chapter Master Banzor,' Guilliman voxed. 'What is your status?'

'The pressure is starting to ease.'

'Can you link up with Empion yet?'

'He will soon,' Empion said. *'We can see you, brother,'* he told Banzor.

'Then we will join you on the slopes, primarch,' Banzor said.

'No,' said Guilliman. 'Break out south. Reinforce Atreus at the next pyramid. What we had hoped to do for you is now your task. March south and end the war on that front.'

Habron broke in. A Thunderhawk transport had *Flame of Illyrium* in its hold as it circled the battlefield. The Techmarine was deploying the scanners of the Explorator from the air. *'Lord Guilliman,'* he said. *'Contact from the Twenty-second.'*

'On the *Cavascor*?'

'No. From beneath the rockslide. Word from Loxias of the 221st. Chapter Master Iasus and some elements of his force have survived.'

'Can they be reached?'

'I am working to determine that. I am not in direct contact with the Chapter Master. Loxias is acting as a relay for as long as he can.'

'Do what you can. If possible, find an extraction point.' On the command network, Guilliman voxed, 'The Twenty-second is still with us. We march to the north, Ultramarines.'

He drove the *Hand of Dominion* through another ork. Its followers stumbled in the shock wave, then died as the *Arbitrator* spoke again. Behind, Guilliman sensed a shift in the rhythms of bolter fire. The legionaries were beginning to counter the attackers coming from the pyramid.

Under the dark grey sky of Thoas, in the light of stars neither setting nor rising, the orks in their thousands rushed through artillery and gunship barrages. A new avalanche, one of flesh and rage, rushed to bury Guilliman.

* * *

Theoretical, Hierax thought, then stopped.

Theoretical, he began again.

His thoughts stuttered, stumbled into formlessness, and looped back. The word revolved through his mind, a refrain without purpose. He stood in the centre of the strategium, his back to the tacticarium table, gazing blankly at a pict screen. He took in nothing from the screen beyond a vague shifting of colours.

Theoretical.

Useless repetition. The dull, cold, hammering toll of grief and anger.

Sirras was gone. Old friend, old comrade, old ally. His belief in Hierax as the proper Chapter Master of the 22nd had been absolute.

His judgement had been flawed.

In the final moments before vox contact with the 22nd had been lost, Hierax had heard Iasus demanding Sirras cease the heavy armour fire. Then the pyramid vanished. The vox went silent. A mountain had fallen.

Hierax mourned his comrade. His anger initially coalesced around Iasus. But Iasus had been correct. Sirras had been the author of his own doom.

Theoretical: Sirras was deficient in his application of reason.

Hierax's thoughts moved out of their spiral. They began to find direction again.

Practical: correct your path where it too closely resembles his.

'Captain?'

Hierax's eyes focused. He looked right. Kletos had entered the strategium. 'What is it, legionary?' Hierax said.

'What we're hearing about the war. Is it true?'

Hierax wondered how long he'd been in a fugue state if there had been time for news of the disaster to spread from the bridge.

'Yes,' Hierax said. '*Yes,*' he snapped. 'The position held by the

Twenty-second has been destroyed. There are no signs as yet of any survivors.'

Kletos swore. 'He should never have been our Chapter Master. We should be down there. If he hadn't–'

'The fault was not that of Chapter Master Iasus,' Hierax said. Kletos fell silent.

'Captain Sirras made an error of judgement, one that he could have avoided had he fully applied our primarch's philosophy.' He knew this to be true. Sirras had been reckless. He had disobeyed an earlier order. Hierax could imagine the situation must have been extreme to push Sirras to make that mistake, but it could not have been the result of applied reason.

'Are we all that remains?' Kletos asked after a moment.

'Perhaps.'

'What are your orders?'

'I will make contact with the primarch. His orders will be mine. I...' He trailed off, his eye caught by the pict screen he had been staring at when Kletos arrived. It displayed the tracked movements and concentrations of the orks. The topography of the map had refreshed itself a few moments before to account for the new physical reality on the planet. Despite the destruction, the ork horde in that position showed very little reduction in density and numbers.

'Why there?' Hierax wondered.

'Captain?' said Kletos.

Hierax pointed at the screen. 'Why are there so many orks here?' Large hordes were attacking the Chapters at the other pyramids, but here was where they were most numerous.

'Chance?' Kletos suggested.

The idea was not unreasonable. Orks were unpredictable partly because their actions were so often dictated by random events. The right topographical dip could change the course of an entire horde's rampage. Even so, the solution felt wrong. 'I don't think so,' Hierax said. 'There have been more orks in this region of the mountain chain from the opening moments of the campaign. There must be something attracting them to the region.'

His eyes widened. With a curse, he turned to a screen on the other side of the strategium. He found what he was looking for immediately.

'Look,' he said to Kletos, tapping the screen with a finger. 'The radiation blooms over that region are anomalously high.'

'You theorise a correlation.'

'I dismiss coincidence, certainly.'

'Why would the radiation levels there be so high?'

'That is the key question.' There were traces along the entire mountain chain, and the reports sent back to the fleet by the Techmarines described evidence pointing to the fortress having fallen in a war. All the signs of damage, though, were many centuries old. The radiation levels around the north pyramid were so high, it was as if the war were not over in that sector. 'Theoretical,' he said. 'There is an ongoing source of radiation somewhere in that vicinity.'

'Caused by the orks?'

'Doubtful. More likely caused by something that is attracting them.' The conjecture crystallised. It gathered weight, becoming a true theoretical. 'Vox!' he called to the bridge. 'I need to speak with Lord Guilliman.'

The shaft ended in a new warren. Iasus wondered how many sub-levels there were. Had the people of Thoas once burrowed as far as the core? These passages were narrower than the ones above, and their ceilings were lower. Many had collapsed too. Some of the damage looked ancient, but much was new. Dust still filled the tunnels. The air grated against Iasus' teeth when he inhaled. The snarls and heavy footsteps of orks echoed everywhere. There were no greenskins at the junction beneath the shaft.

Burrus was the first to join him. He looked around, listening. 'Are we surrounded?' he asked.

'We may well be,' Iasus said. 'They infest these passages.'

'Are they looking for us?'

'I don't think so. I don't think they know we're here. Though they will before long.'

'Why are they here?' Burrus moved to one side as more and more of the company dropped from the ladder and out of the shaft.

'Perhaps heading for other combat zones. They know these tunnels well, after all.'

'*Chapter Master,*' said Loxias. '*I have made contact. The rest of the Legion knows you're alive.*'

'Well done, brother. Are there orders?'

'*Lord Guilliman wants you to pull out.*'

'We would like nothing more. Is he aware of our situation?'

'*He is. I am attempting to find a path for you.*'

'Your sensors can reach this far?'

'*Hardly. But in conjunction with the explorator augury web of First Company, we can guess better.*' Loxias went quiet. His voice was growing weaker. At each silence, Iasus wondered if no more would be said. He was about to call the Techmarine's name when Loxias spoke again. '*I have a possible route,*' he said. '*Head south-east of your current position. A crevasse was opened during the rockslide.*'

'Can you be more precise?'

'*The tunnels are a maze here. Many have collapsed and the ground remains unstable. Getting an accurate reading of what is intact is beyond our means. The crevasse is a long one, though. If you keep to the heading, you should encounter it.*'

'All right. Thank you, brother. Courage and honour.'

'*Courage and honour, Chapter Master.*'

The remains of the 221st headed south-east. The route was broken. Tunnels crossed and twisted. They ended suddenly in heaps of fallen stone, and the Ultramarines doubled back. The sounds of the orks grew louder. The growls bounced and echoed, growing louder. These orks were closer, though there was no way to tell where they were or how many. They seemed to be an infestation, vermin filling the veins of Thoas.

Iasus reached an intersection running east and west. He turned east. He saw orks a hundred feet down. They carried crude promethium torches to light their way. The space stank of fumes and greenskin musk. These orks were not just passing through to a battle. They had been in this sector a long time. They had some reason to wish to be deep below the surface.

The orks saw the Ultramarines.

'They're in our way,' Iasus said.

Bolter fire slammed into the greenskins. The two forces raced towards each other. As Iasus plunged his power sword into the nearest ork, he wondered how long he and his Chapter would continue to move forwards. There would no longer be a question of holding the line.

The Ultramarines would advance, or they would die.

'I'm listening,' Guilliman said to Hierax. He had his back to a large boulder. The *Hand of Dominion* punched an ork with such force the greenskin exploded, drenching the area with a spray of liquefied flesh and vaporised blood. He put shells through the chests of another three, leaving holes the size of his fist. The killing was automatic. He could steal a few seconds from the march forwards to hear what the captain of the Destroyers had to say.

'Your sector shows abnormally high radiation levels along with the most significant concentration of orks. The tunnel network also goes much deeper than we suspected, beyond our ability to scan. Deduction – the source of the radiation is also the lure for the orks. The network, furthermore, is a former military installation. Theoretical – there is a large cache of weapons beneath the surface near your location.'

'What is your practical, captain?'

'Deployment of the Second Destroyers to find and secure the weapons, while intervening on behalf of our Chapter Master.'

'Agreed,' Guilliman said. He could almost hear Hierax's look of surprise through the vox. 'Deploy via drop pod to the coordinates Habron will supply. Wait for my authorisation before descending into the complex.'

'By your command,' Hierax said, and signed off.

Why have you authorised this? Guilliman asked himself. He turned and punched the boulder behind him. The explosion hurled large, jagged pieces of shrapnel in all directions, impaling and crushing more orks. He moved into the space he had opened up, then headed north again, marching in lock step once more with the Invictarii.

I authorised the deployment because reason calls for it, he thought. *A fresh company will reinforce our efforts and secure the survival of the rest of the Twenty-second Chapter. I authorised it because Hierax specifically referred to his Chapter Master. I authorised it because Hierax's proposed mission is one of recovery, not annihilation. I authorised it because the captain of the Second Destroyers is capable of reflection. His deductions are sound. He has theorised well.*

I authorised the deployment because it was rational and needful.

Ork bullets thudded against his armour from behind. He turned to see that a mob of the beasts had made a concerted charge and overwhelmed the legionaries at his rear. Two lay still. Three others were fighting for their lives, being borne down by the blows from heavy chainaxes. He fired into the attackers and headed back. He drove the power gauntlet into the ground just before he reached the struggle. The ground bucked. Debris flew. The ripple through the earth knocked the orks off-balance. That was enough for the legionaries to rise and enact their vengeance.

Why did you authorise Hierax? Guilliman thought again. He was not satisfied with his answers, though they were correct and true. He marched up the slope once more, shooting into the green tide.

I authorised it because of a hunch, he admitted.

He thought Hierax was right. He did not know what weapons they would find, yet already he suspected they would be foul. If that were true, the Destroyers' expertise would be useful.

But why?

There was a deeper instinct. A suspicion that he refused to name. He sensed it at the back of his mind, lurking at the edge of consciousness, threatening to form out of the fog of half-thoughts and demand to be articulated.

He turned away from it. The suspicion was unprofitable. It served no purpose. It never would unless it became a reality. Until then, his conscious reasons for deploying the Second Destroyers were enough.

Relentless, the suspicion pounded at the wall he erected. It called to him from the other side. It demanded to be heard.

You will not like what waits below.

That war is a means, not an end, is a harmful truism. Only the most consciously perverse have ever maintained that war was their end. Even then, the degree to which they believe their assertion is debatable. There were moments when I thought Gallan might not have any purpose beyond the destruction he caused. The collapse of order in the streets of Macragge Civitas did, at first glance, provide evidence of conflict for its own sake. But a dispassionate examination of Gallan's actions reveals the opposite. Though his tactics were ill-advised, governed far more by anger than by analysis of any rigour, they still had a clear purpose – the suppression of opposition to his regime, and the elimination of even the desire to oppose him. So it is with all warriors. War has a purpose.

Yet a still deeper examination reveals the very dangerous fallacy shored up by this logic. Gallan had a goal, but the effect of his tactics far exceeded what was intended, and ultimately worked against that goal. He created a situation that, had it been permitted to continue, would have engendered perpetual violence. It would have been necessary for him to maintain the rule of terror and violence to eliminate opposition whether such opposition existed or not.

This, then, is the great risk of war. Its power is so great, it can easily become self-sustaining. The stated ends become rationalisations, in effect the means to the goal of endless war. The prospect of the imminent conclusion to my Father's Great Crusade fills some of my brothers with melancholy. I understand and, to a degree, share in this reaction. But I know enough to be wary of it. It gives me a greater, more profound pleasure to contemplate the fact that, our work done, we will have gifted humanity with a true end to war.

– Guilliman, *Reflections: Third Fragment*, xxxii

EIGHT

SONS AND DESTROYERS • PRECISION • THE LAST DESCENT

As Guilliman's march moved north, the gunships moved their strafing runs to the south. A barrier of fire rose between the Ultramarines and the pyramid. The tide had turned completely now. The orks emerging from the tunnels no longer streamed towards the pyramid. Many still came from that structure, and ran straight into the Thunderhawks' fire. The artillery barrage from Guilliman's long-range guns was now aimed at the base of the exposed peak, hitting the orks as they swarmed out of the tunnels.

Gage voxed, *'Is it my imagination or are we finally thinning their numbers?'*

'I think we are,' Guilliman said. There were still thousands of orks. They covered the slope. But Gage was right. They did not appear to be reinforced by an inexhaustible resupply. The Ultramarines at last were killing the orks faster than the greenskins could summon reinforcements.

The drop pods came down within a hundred yards of the targeted crevasse. They punched shallow craters in the rubble of the slide. They crushed and incinerated scores of orks clambering over the rocks to get to Guilliman's line. The hatches blew open, and the Destroyers entered the field.

The mob of orks caught between the First Chapter's infantry and the 22nd Chapter's Destroyers survived less than five minutes. The two lines of Ultramarines advanced to meet each other through the bodies of the greenskins.

When the last of the mob went down under a hail of shells, Guilliman looked at the legionaries before him. *These too are my sons*, he reminded himself. He needed to. There was a distance between him and the Destroyers. They were a necessary unit, but they were an imperfect fit with his vision of the Ultramarines. Even their armour marked them as separate. It was black. The blue of the XIII Legion was present on their pauldrons and in a single vertical stripe down the centre of their helms, but almost nowhere else. Guilliman had noticed the same approach to colours in the Destroyers of Fulgrim and Corvus' Legions, as if they had more in common with members of the same specialisation than with their brother legionaries. It was an impression he did not want reinforced into a reality. This was why Guilliman had made Iasus Chapter Master of the 22nd. He would set a tone more in keeping with the other Chapters of the Legion.

Many of the Destroyers wore raptor icons suspended from the belts at their waists. The birds of prey were another mark of difference. They were reminders that their bearers had come from Terra. The face of the Legion was changing, but far more slowly in the Second Destroyers.

Hierax had brought the entire company, as far as Guilliman could tell, with the exception of the heavy support. One of the drop pods had even brought the Dreadnought Laevius. Guilliman had noticed that the ancient warrior had killed orks using only his power fist.

What is your cannon armed with? he wondered.

He saw many armaments that made him grimace with distaste. He knew, without asking, that the missiles of the rocket launchers were radiation weapons. This was the identity of the

Destroyers. It was why they existed. He had not disbanded them. He had never banned their way of war. But he had removed them from the standard conduct of the wars of the XIII Legion. They were last resorts. They must be so, for they left poisoned ruin in their wake. They were the warriors of extinction and extermination.

But the rad and bio-alchem weapons were holstered or slung over their backs. They had killed the orks with bolter fire. Guilliman saw, and appreciated the respect they showed him. They had come to do their duty, not push their agenda.

Hierax walked ahead of his company. He removed his helmet and stood before Guilliman. 'We are ready to do what you need of us,' he said.

'You are welcome to this field,' said Guilliman. 'And to the aid of your Chapter Master.' He looked at Hierax's bald, war-ravaged features, and saw the pride of duty that shone through them.

'We are eager to join him,' Hierax said. He looked past Guilliman. 'Victory on this battlefield is close at hand, I see.'

The legionaries of the First Chapter had established a perimeter on the south side of the crevasse. They were holding the orks back. There was no break in their fire. Nothing could approach from the south without being turned into bleeding meat. Hierax was right. The ranks of the orks had thinned noticeably in the last few minutes. They were scattered across the slope. They were still attacking, but they could not muster a concentrated charge. Very few managed to come near enough to require a legionary to use his blade instead of his bolter. Upslope, to the east, the stream of orks coming from the exposed tunnels had slowed to a trickle. The battle on this side of the pyramid was effectively over.

Guilliman frowned. He knew how many he and his sons had killed. There were too few orks. 'Habron,' he voxed, 'what is the situation south of our position?'

'The consolidations are successful. The other Chapters are beginning the process of extermination.'

'So where have the orks gone?'

'As some of the hordes withdraw, they also diminish in size,' Habron said.

'So they're going back underground.'

'Apparently.'

Guilliman turned to Hierax. 'Your hypothesis is gathering credibility by the second. The orks are abandoning the field and returning to the tunnels. The surviving Twenty-second cannot be that powerful a lure. Something else is calling them.'

Hierax glanced at the crevasse. 'If the withdrawal began when we took this location…'

Guilliman nodded. 'They see that we intend to descend.'

'Theoretical,' Hierax said. 'The orks are desperate to stop our move into the deep tunnels. Their prize is there, and of gigantic importance to them.'

'Practical,' Guilliman responded. 'We shall do what they most fear.'

The descent began a few minutes later. Guilliman took a third of his infantry below, leaving the Invictarii to command the rest and direct the final annihilation of the orks at the surface. Gage led the legionaries of the First Chapter. Guilliman marched with the Second Destroyers. He gave Hierax and his troops the honour of being at the front of the rescue of the battered 22nd Chapter. They would also know he was watching.

They too are my sons.

They must know this too, and all that comes with being of my blood.

The sides of the crevasse were steep, but along its length, as it widened gradually, there was a fall of rubble creating a drop just gradual enough for the Ultramarines to use it as a path to the depths. Even Laevius could manoeuvre his ponderous bulk down, his power fist smashing larger boulders to dust along the way.

'Have you pinpointed the position of the Twenty-second?' Guilliman asked Habron as the march began.

'The signals still lack precision. My best estimate is that they are at a level approximately equal to halfway down the crevasse.'

'Then we will enter the tunnels there, and trust to come within range of Captain Iasus' vox transmissions.'

'He will be grateful for your swift arrival,' Habron said.

'That bad?'

'Based on his last message, yes.'

They annihilated the first ork contingent. But three junctions on, the greenskins stopped the 22nd's advance. Iasus had no idea how far the crevasse was from his Chapter's current position. It didn't matter. *We aren't going any further.* The junction was a tangle of narrow tunnels, heading off in half a dozen directions. The orks came out of all of them. Their snarls were expressions of absolute rage. There was no joy of battle now.

Giants led the charge, orks so large they had to hunch forwards or scrape their skulls against the ceiling. They wielded chain-axes and cleavers so huge they chopped through walls. They tramped smaller orks in their rush to engage the Ultramarines.

Bellowing, powerful as a flesh Dreadnought, a monster charged at Iasus. He jumped back from the axe's swing. He pumped the ork full of mass-reactive shells. Blood jetted, drenching him. The beast kept coming. It brought its axe in again, low and from the side. There would be no evasion. Iasus swung his power sword at the weapon. He sliced through the chain and the edge of the blade. The whiplash of the chain spoiled the blow, tilting the blade. It hit him at an angle, the main force of the hit crushing instead of cutting. The axe smashed him against the side of the wall, gouged a chunk out of his armour and sank through his carapace and into his fused ribs. Bone cracked. His blood mixed with the ork's.

The ork grunted and pulled the axe free. It raised the weapon over its head. Iasus shook off his stun and lunged upwards with his sword. The blade's energy seared the air as it plunged through flesh. Iasus drove it up beneath the ork's chin and out through its crown. Its jaw sagged. Its small, furious eyes went dim. Its arms trembled a moment longer as if the corpse sought to complete that final strike. Then the huge mass collapsed.

Iasus withdrew the sword and stepped back. There was another giant brute behind the first. Others had forced their way past his right flank while he fought. They were working their way down the tunnel, pushing the Ultramarines back, dismembering them with colossal blows. They absorbed bolter shells as if they were hewn from the mountain itself. Burrus had lost his left hand. Cursing, he slashed at the ork with his chainsword. Behind him, still another monster had smashed a legionary's helmet and skull with a stone hammer that must have weighed half a tonne.

'Back!' Iasus shouted. He threw himself right, away from the cleaver of his new attacker and put a burst of six shells through the forehead of Burrus' foe. 'Twenty paces back and east!' They had passed a space where several walls had fallen, one knocking the next down, turning several adjoining tunnels into a large cavern. There was space there to form up and hit the orks with combined fire.

The Ultramarines retreated. The orks came at them with lumbering fury. They felled two more brothers with blows that crushed and severed. At the gap, the 22nd contracted into a massed square, a dozen legionaries in length, two rows deep, one crouching, the other standing. The orks circled, trying to find a gap, failing and charging anyway, to be burned and shot by multiple bolters and flamers. The boiling river of smaller orks flowed behind the giants, shrieking their anger. Some, in their need to kill, streamed between the monsters. They were brought down, but the shells they absorbed gave the huge brutes the chance to reach closer and land blows before the sheer hail of ordnance and jets of flaming promethium dropped them.

'I think we've done something to upset them,' Burrus hissed between gritted teeth as he fired. He was crouched before Iasus. He had maglocked his chainsword to his wrist and was wielding his bolter one-handed. His stump no longer bled.

'Our presence has triggered something,' Iasus said. 'Do you sense it, brothers?' he voxed. 'Do you smell the stench from the greenskins? It's desperation!'

'If they're that desperate for us to leave,' Burrus said, 'they could have simply stepped aside.'

Iasus grunted in amusement. 'Reloading,' he said, and Burrus unleashed a long burst.

The legionaries were in a good position. They could hold the orks for some time.

But that would be all. There would be no more advancing, not against a horde this size. Iasus accepted the truth of the situation. This space was where the 22nd would end. He tried raising Loxias on the vox. The Techmarine had fallen silent.

Iasus sensed the coming of change before he heard it. The movement of the orks altered. It became even more frantic. There was confusion, too, he thought. Instead of the constant, frothing circle, there were counter-currents as some orks sought to push their way back out of the chamber.

The vox crackled to life. *'Chapter Master Iasus,'* said a voice.

The voice. Deep, resonant, calm with the authority of the absolute strategist. It was the voice of true nobility. Iasus had witnessed the false kind on Macragge. He had been there to see the misrule of Gallan. He had seen the ambitious and the proud seek to raise themselves above their kin, and in so doing corrupt themselves, make themselves into things of contempt. The true nobility did not need to prove itself. It simply *was*, a fact as indisputable as the orbit of planets and the majesty of stars.

'Lord Guilliman,' Iasus said. He wondered if he was giving in to a false hope. In the chaos of snarls and gunfire, perhaps he had imagined hearing his name.

The voice spoke again, and it was real.

'We are coming to relieve you, Chapter Master,' Guilliman said. *'I think it unnecessary to ask if you are the one who has excited the greenskins to such a degree.'*

'We have had an effect on them, it is true.'

'Hold fast, Iasus. We will be there soon.'

'Legionaries of the Twenty-second,' Iasus voxed, grinning. 'Our primarch approaches. Courage and honour!'

'Courage and honour!'

Iasus was sure the bolter shells flew with greater energy and force. Huge bodies exploded. Ork warlords reduced to slabs of stinking flesh hit the floor, shaking the stone. The monsters howled with greater and greater fury, greater and greater desperation. A few moments later, Iasus heard a series of deep, booming concussions. The orks heard them too. Even the largest turned at the sound. A great bell was tolling, and it was coming for the greenskins.

The concussions came closer, shaking dust from the ceiling. There was gunfire too, and the sharp, destructive blast of grenades. The sounds came from the south, to Iasus' left. The sounds of the ork horde changed there. The desperation reached a new level of intensity. The rage surpassed all reason.

'Is that… *panic?*' Burrus asked.

Iasus wondered the same. He did not think orks were capable of panic, not in human terms. If it was not panic he heard, then he lacked the word to describe the phenomenon. The howling was higher pitched. It was so all-consuming it seemed as if the throats making that sound should have torn themselves open.

A few paces from Iasus, the two largest orks glared at him, then turned south. They hefted their weapons, chainaxes so thick they could have been hammers. They roared, and the smaller brutes they commanded began to turn away from the 22nd.

The orks did not have a chance to leave. The concussion arrived. Guilliman arrived. The primarch emerged from the darkness of the tunnels, bearing light and death. His left fist was bathed in cerulean and scarlet energy. The muzzles of his combi-bolter flashed, explosive death bursting from the barrels. He punched the nearest of the ork giants. The greenskin towered over Guilliman, yet it seemed to Iasus the primarch's head touched the ceiling, and it was the ork who had to look upwards in the split second before it vanished, torn asunder by the discharge of the power gauntlet.

Guilliman was relentless, but it was the precision of his relentlessness that stunned Iasus. He believed without question in the Imperial Truth, and in the philosophy of pure reason espoused by Guilliman. But now, as he watched Guilliman fight, he saw the absolute precision of each movement. Blow, sidestep, trigger pull, a sweeping gesture around the falling hulk to smash the next – every act occurred because reason said it must, in the order dictated by reason. Iasus witnessed the perfection of precision, and he understood at last the resilient mortal need to believe in the divine.

Guilliman killed the last of the giant orks in the chamber within the first ten seconds of his arrival. The lesser orks screamed their horror. They attacked him all the same, and they died even more quickly. Moments behind Guilliman came the Second Destroyers. They entered the cavern like the march of night. They killed with excess, pouring more shells than were necessary into the foe, reducing every enemy to unrecognisable pulp. The orks were caught now between Iasus' formation, Guilliman and Hierax's company.

By the time legionaries of the First Chapter arrived with Marius Gage, there was nothing left to kill.

Hierax approached Iasus. He removed his helmet and saluted. 'I am glad to find you well, Chapter Master,' he said.

'I'm glad to hear you say so.' Iasus meant the remark as a jest. He saw Hierax wince.

'I am sorry for our Chapter's great losses,' the Destroyer captain said.

'As am I,' said Iasus. 'The fallen will be honoured.'

Hierax lowered his head in solemn agreement, then looked up. 'Their mistakes will also be studied.'

'You believe so?'

'When the consequences are so grave, the study is vital.'

Iasus clasped Hierax's pauldron. 'At the same time, a life given to service must not be reduced to one error.' *Sirras' name will not become synonymous with folly,* Iasus thought.

'Thank you, Chapter Master,' Hierax said.

Guilliman appeared at Hierax's shoulder. The captain stepped aside. 'Legionary Burrus says the orks became uncharacteristically desperate to halt your advance,' he said to Iasus.

'Yes, they did.'

'Did their distress grow worse when you advanced in a particular direction?'

Iasus thought through the beats of the battle. 'Yes,' he realised. 'When we moved south-east of here.'

'Show me,' Guilliman said.

They found the ramp a hundred yards beyond the last position the 22nd had reached before the orks turned them back. Past a major junction, the southern branch widened. The tunnel was as large as the ones in the upper levels of the pyramids and mountains. It dropped at a steep gradient, though Guilliman judged that it was still within the capabilities of most vehicles to climb. The northern branch was filled with rubble, but it too was broad. Had it been clear, Guilliman suspected he would have seen a ramp going up towards the surface.

The descending path turned sharply every few hundred yards, doubling back on itself. It was a colossal switchback heading down to the roots of the mountains. Ork snarls echoed from the depths. This far away the sound of the horde was a low grumble of thunder.

'We know where they have gone,' he said. He had brought his commanders forwards. He, Gage, Iasus and Hierax marched together at the head of the column.

'There must be entrances at the base of the cordillera too,' Iasus said. 'We noted the horde appear to shrink at one moment.'

'Likely so,' Guilliman agreed. 'The question, then, is what is so important to the orks.' He turned to Hierax. 'This is your hypothesis, captain. Extrapolate.'

'Weapons,' Hierax told Iasus. 'They would account for the radiation levels of this region and the orks' interest. This too.' He gestured at the ramp. 'A means to transport large quantities of something quickly below the surface.'

'Interesting the creators of the tunnels did not use one of their shafts,' Gage said.

'For very large quantities of ordnance, for example, this would be faster. Entire convoys of transporters could take this route.'

After a minute, Iasus said, 'What kind of weapons?'

'I would be speculating rather than extrapolating.'

'Do so,' Guilliman said. He knew the answer. He suspected Iasus did too. The long-term radiation was the key. He wanted Hierax to say the words, though. There must be a unity of presumptions across his force.

'Rad missiles, or something very like them,' Hierax said. 'At the least.'

'What use would they be to the orks?' Iasus asked. 'The

greenskins would never be capable of figuring out how to launch them.'

'True,' Guilliman said. 'That does not rule out the possibility of a catastrophic accident.'

'Why rad missiles?' Gage said. He seemed to be speaking to himself more than to the others. 'Against whom? We haven't found any trace of who the creators of this fortress complex had as an enemy.'

No one answered. Guilliman sensed the answer waited below. If there were weapons there, they would be the only artefacts beyond the fading murals to have survived the civilisation's disappearance. Their presence made the presence of other relics more likely.

You will not like the answer. That voice, a dark intuition that shunned the principles of reason, gnawed at his peace of mind.

The ramp dropped further and further, back and forth, hundreds of yards in one direction, then hundreds in the other, dropping a full mile, two, then three. The ork rage rose to meet them, ever louder. There were thousands waiting below, guarding something they could never use. *This is the heart of your empire*, Guilliman wanted to tell them. *In the end, this is what you will fight to own. Your extermination will be a mercy for you as well. Your purpose is empty.*

The ramp turned back on itself one last time. It carried on several hundred yards more, then levelled off and turned sharply to the right into a huge opening, the largest Guilliman had seen in the complex. It glowed with a dull crimson light, flickering, irregularly pulsing. The orks were there, spilling out of the entrance, their rage shaking cavern walls. The green tide had become a wall.

'My sons,' said Guilliman, 'let us end this war.'

Could we have foreseen it? We will never escape that question. Even those of my brothers who might une-quivocally answer no will still have that question circle back to them, to be dealt with again and again. Could I have foreseen it? I should have. I had the lesson of Gallan. I should have understood the consequences of Monarchia. I had other chances too. The evidence was before me. There were inferences to be made. But I did not see. The precise nature of my blindness is what I still work to determine. I will not succumb to the temptation to say the correct analysis will prevent another such tragedy. There can never be another. The worst has happened, and the best is gone forever.

– Guilliman, journal entry, 120.M31

NINE

TREASURE • THRONE • MIST

Guilliman drove the *Hand of Dominion* through the ork before him. The blow disintegrated the brute immediately behind. Guilliman fired the *Arbitrator* through the gap, and created a larger one. He parted the wall of orks, and moved that much closer to the centre of the chamber. Behind him, his sons advanced at a steady pace, destroying all flesh before them. The advance into the cavern was not a charge. The gunfire could not be indiscriminate.

There could be no absence of precision. Not here. The orks attacked with no thought of the place they were so bent on retaining. The Ultramarines column gave them a target for their crude slugs. The legionaries absorbed the hits and marched on in a straight light through the centre of the cavern. They did not take shelter. There was none to take.

Theoretical: the possibility of accidental detonation is slight, or it would have happened long ago.

Practical: do not put that analysis to the test unnecessarily.

The cavern's ceiling was over three hundred feet high. The mural that had once covered it was almost completely blackened by smoke. The space was enormous, and the orks had erected

huge, patchwork metal icons across the floor and on every level
of decking. Snarling grotesques loomed over the Ultramarines.
Torch flames waved between their gaping jaws. Piles of debris
rose fifty feet or more. The orks capered and howled and fired
from their peaks. They swarmed over the hills of scrap and detri-
tus, shrieking war and outrage. Many were massive brutes, as
large as the ones that had cornered Iasus' survivors of the 22nd.
They lumbered forwards now for a final assault, determined to
keep what was theirs.

The orks' treasures lined the perimeter of the chamber. They
rested in pyramidal stacks on decks projecting from the walls.
They waited in adamantium crates nesting one on top of the
other in towers thirty feet high. They were missiles, bombs,
rockets and shells. The largest of the missiles were the size of
Deathstrikes. The shells could arm a Baneblade tank.

The icons on the armaments were as unfamiliar to Guilliman as the others he had seen in the fortress. The shapes of
the weapons were not. Standard Template Construct technology
had once been in use on Thoas. The STCs themselves might be
long gone, but their terrible work remained. The shapes of the
missiles told him much. The crimson icons, enough of them
still visible beneath the ork vandalism, were clear warnings.

And in the first minutes of the assault on the cavern, Dymas,
the Techmarine of the Second Destroyers, confirmed Guilliman's
suspicions. His auspex scan picked up the trace elements in the
atmosphere. Over the centuries, the monstrous weapons in the
storage site had tainted the air, as if the darkness of their way
of war were contagious.

'*The radiation spike is extreme,*' Dymas said. '*Rad weapons of all
types. The shells are primarily phosphex. Some are bio-alchem. So
are some of the missiles.*'

'Can you identify the type?' Guilliman asked.

'*No. In addition, some of the readings are confusing.*'

Theoretical – there are weapons here that combine some of all of these characteristics.'

Guilliman fired again, picking up speed as he blasted the orks from his path. He grimaced in distaste. These were the weapons of last resort, stored in such quantity they seemed to be instead this civilisation's weapons of choice. His reluctant intuition was proving correct. He did not like the revelation of this cavern. What kind of a culture was he rediscovering for Imperial history?

The orks could not use the technology, yet they recognised enormous destructive power. Somehow, in the century or more in which they had made Thoas theirs, they had not triggered their own destruction. It was as if the weapons would not deign to be expended in so mundane a fashion. Around the stockpiles were greenskin assemblages that were part workshop, part altar. They celebrated the great weapons and tried to construct their own. Stunted, crooked missiles stood in a ragged cluster before the rows of monsters. Orkish shells were piled high before their models. *It is*, Guilliman thought, *as if the orks hope their creations will absorb the mysterious power of the relics they have found simply by being in close proximity to them.*

The orks did more than mimic the things they had found. They sought to use them. Even if they could never be successful, they would try until death. It was the result of their efforts that Guilliman rushed towards. It was in the centre of the cavern, and it was the centre of the ork empire. It was the heart of the madness, and the soul of barbaric war.

The throne of destruction towered over everything else in the cavern. The orks had constructed it by piling up ordnance. Missiles, rockets, bombs and shells formed a giant heap. It was a mound more than a throne, a mountain of crawling, burning, agonising death. The ork emperor sat at the peak. There was no design to the hill, though Guilliman could see how the ruling greenskin had shaped the pile to conform to its bulk. It was huge, bloated with muscle and savage greed. It was twice the size of any ork Guilliman had seen on Thoas. It was as broad as a Dreadnought. It wore a crown made of the deadly shells. Its armour was a piston-driven framework of iron and steam. Pipes higher than the monster's head spewed flame. Strapped to its legs and its arms were more shells. Its hide was a mass of scars and burns.

The seat of empire, Guilliman thought. This ork existed at what it believed to be a pinnacle. It exalted itself in its fury. Guilliman stared at a grotesque being ruling a gutted empire from the top of a construct of ruin. It had to be exterminated.

The extermination had to be total.

'Captain Hierax,' Guilliman voxed. 'Destroy the greenskins by any means necessary. Do you understand?'

'I do, Lord Guilliman.'

The ork stood when it saw Guilliman. It opened its maw wide and roared a challenge. It took two ponderous steps down from its throne.

Guilliman butchered his way through the last of the greenskins between him and the huge mound. The surrounding horde screamed at him, but the lesser orks did not follow as he started to climb the hill.

He half expected the shells to roll and shift when he set foot on the slope. The heap was surprisingly stable. It would have to be, Guilliman thought, not to collapse under the weight of the beast. The ordnance appeared to have been stacked at random. Perhaps it had been, but the casings of the shells and bombs and rockets had been welded to each other.

The mountain was an act of insanity, Guilliman thought. *Or perhaps faith.* The perfect exemplar of the equivalence of the two words.

As he climbed, he removed the *Hand of Dominion*. He could not use it on this throne. If he struck the weapons, the gauntlet's energy field would disrupt the matter of their casings. He would unleash what the orks had somehow failed to. He would not complete the former civilisation's madness. He maglocked the *Hand of Dominion* to his belt and took up the *Gladius Incandor* once again.

Precision, he thought. That was the only route to victory here. Every blow must be deliberately placed. There could be no error.

The ork emperor charged down the slope. It wielded an immense chain hammer. The head of the weapon was a huge lumpen mass. Multiple chains whirled around it. Guilliman eyed the weapon, and pictured what it could do to the wrong target with that much power behind its blows.

Practical: strategic sacrifice will be necessary.

Guilliman leapt up to meet his foe. They clashed at the midpoint of the mountain. The ork swung the hammer one-handed. Guilliman fired at the weapon's head. The shells of the *Arbitrator* punched craters into the dense metal. One of the chains broke and flew off, a spinning scythe of teeth. It sliced into the ork's face, opening a diagonal wound from its left eye to the right of its lower jaw. The ork bellowed. It smashed its left fist against Guilliman's flank, slamming him against the head of the hammer. He gasped. It was like being crushed between walls. Pain sparked along his frame.

He had expected it, and he had already adjusted his strike, adding more force to compensate for the shock and the wound. *Incandor* slashed through the framework of the ork's armour and the tendons of its left arm. The limb sagged. The beast snarled. With a brutish form of warrior's pride, it hit back with its wounded arm. Instead of blocking, Guilliman absorbed the blow. The servo-motors of his armour whined in protest at the speed of his movement, and still the ork knocked him off his feet. He fell against the weapons. Welding gave way, and now the casings did shift. The ork reached him in a single stride.

The next move in the battle became clear. Guilliman delayed rising, and so the ork did what he wished. It used both hands to raise the hammer high over its head. It was preparing a killing blow.

A blow that cost it seconds.

Guilliman shoved himself up and to the right, up the slope, scattering explosives. Shells rolled down the slope, a foretaste of a dreadful avalanche. The hammer came down. It plunged deep into the throne. Shells exploded. Fire and shrapnel sprayed Guilliman and the emperor. Hunched, the ork yanked at the wedged hammer. Guilliman leapt. Level with the ork's head, he plunged *Incandor* into the beast's right eye. It howled and jerked its head back, stumbling a step down the slope. It swung the hammer wildly.

Contingency, chance, luck. The perversities of war that were the cancer on any rational strategy. They served the ork in this moment. The hammer struck Guilliman as he landed. It hit him on the shoulders and drove him down into the mound. His pauldrons cracked wide. His spine ignited with sulphurous agony. The surface gave way completely beneath his right leg and he had no leverage. He put all of his weight on his left leg and lunged out of the depression just as the ork recovered its balance and aimed another blow at him.

Guilliman had no choice. This time he could not let the blow connect. He sidestepped left. The hammer dislodged more shells. A tremor shook the mound. The shock of each impact spread through the construct. The welds were the weak point, and broke first. Guilliman and the ork stood on a leviathan that was slowly waking to rolling life.

Below, the chamber was a sea of coordinated bolter fire. The 22nd and the Destroyers were forcing the green tide to recede.

Guilliman moved into the ork's blind side, reaching in to strike with *Incandor*. He held the *Arbitrator* ready, but pulled the trigger only when he was sure of the shell's trajectory. He fired into the central mass of the beast, blowing away its armour plating and stitching explosions across the monster's chest, but it was too consumed by its hate for him to notice.

The ork wound up for another two-handed strike with the hammer, this time from the side.

Analysis.

Seeing the arc of the coming blow, its force and its consequences in a microsecond.

Do not absorb this blow.

Do not let it strike the mound.

Guilliman charged the ork, ramming his shoulders into its torso. The beast was too huge to topple, but he was now too close for the ork to hit him with its hammer. It dropped the weapon and grabbed Guilliman with its claws. It lifted him from the ground, squeezing with a strength that could powder granite. It lifted him high, bellowing in triumph. The vice of absolute brutish strength tightened around his torso. Even with its primitive armour damaged, the ork had the power to crush him in seconds.

The monster knew it had won. It held him like a trophy, savouring the moment of destruction.

These were seconds during which the ork did not move. It did not evade.

They were the seconds Guilliman needed.

The seconds he had foreseen.

His arms were free. He brought up the *Arbitrator* and fired a sustained burst into the ork's face. The remaining eye burst. The jaw disintegrated. Guilliman fired into the maw and the neck exploded. The skull drooped, and the crown of shells fell off. Guilliman kept firing, straight down through the head, the shells stopped by the huge mass of the body, detonating in the ork, never reaching the stacked ordnance.

The ork's grip loosened, but it held him for almost five seconds after he had reduced its head to a gelatinous mass of bone fragments. At last the arms fell away. Guilliman landed on the shells. The mound shifted again. The huge body fell. It rolled and slid down the slope. The mass of armaments began to lose coherence, slumping forwards through the cavern.

At the sight of their murdered emperor, the orks despaired. They cried out in anguish and confusion. Guilliman strode down from the fallen throne, sending death before him. The surviving greenskins fled.

The horde flowed out of the cavern. The orks abandoned their icons and their unusable treasures. They sought the strength in their numbers. They followed a channel Hierax had left open to them, out of the cavern.

Guilliman walked through the cavern, shooting at the fleeing enemy, picturing what would be happening beyond the entrance. On the ramp, there would be thousands of orks now. They would fill the space. Their ferocity would turn them around. They would attack again.

Which was what Hierax wanted them to do.

By any means necessary, Guilliman thought. *I have decreed what will happen now. I accept it.*

These too are my sons.

Guilliman neared the entrance as Laevius' autocannon arm launched rad-poisoned shells into the front lines of the orks. While the forward portion of the horde milled in confusion and blood, the Destroyers launched some of the very rockets the orks had so long claimed as their own. At last, they witnessed the power within.

The rockets burst in the air above the horde, releasing the green mist of phosphex. It ignited and fell on the orks. White-green flame writhed like a wounded animal. The orks shrieked in agony. The horde boiled with panic and sought to flee. The rapid movement attracted the phosphex, spreading it wider and wider. Metal dissolved. Flesh burned to bone. The greenskins vanished in a growing conflagration.

Guilliman watched the expansion of crawling, atrocious death. It took a long time for the horde to burn. Where the mist had fallen, the ground would be tainted forever. This sector of the ruins would be rendered unusable.

Guilliman found the idea of the permanent loss of Thoas' heritage no longer troubled him as it once had.

So he was not surprised when Gage voxed, *'There is something you must see.'*

EPILOGUE

ERASURE

The chamber was a smaller one, reached through the back of the main cavern. Gage's infantry had found it while wiping out the orks that had remained behind the throne and tried to fight. The space was choked with debris, but had apparently held little interest for the greenskins. Gage had noticed there was another intact mural visible behind the piles of discarded metal, and had ordered the room cleared.

Gage, Iasus and Hierax waited at the threshold. Guilliman stood in the centre of the chamber. He turned slowly, absorbing the details of the mural.

'I don't understand,' Gage said. 'Some of the uniforms are the same as the ones we saw near the more southern pyramids, but the representation is completely different.'

'*Different* is not fully accurate, Marius,' Guilliman said. 'They are *opposed*.'

The same martial style to the art was present here. The same type of heroic figures. These, though, wore uniforms heavy in rich, violet sashes. They stood on the corpses of their foes, which wore the colours of the heroes depicted elsewhere in the complex.

Guilliman's hands tightened into fists. 'We were wondering what this fortress was made to defend, and who it was meant to keep out,' he said. 'We did not consider the enemies were already inside.' He turned to the Chapter Masters and the captain. 'Whatever civilisation once existed elsewhere on Thoas, it is long gone. In the end, all that remained is this fortress, and it was riven, at war with itself.'

'The signs of bombardment to the south...' Gage said.

Guilliman nodded. 'The bombardment came from here. Likely bio-alchem weapons, since the taint has passed.'

'Madness to have fought with such weapons at such close quarters,' Hierax said.

'Exactly,' said Guilliman. 'We see the result.' Hierax was right. The war was madness. The way in which this civilisation destroyed itself was beyond obscene. He had landed on Thoas expecting the ruins to show some sign of a heroic last stand against xenos invaders. Instead, here was a vision of humanity given over to a folly so profound he could find no words for his disgust.

'Captain Hierax,' he said. 'You and your company will take custody of the armament in this cavern. You will remove them from Thoas, and take them into our arsenals.' To Gage he said, 'Once we are sure the orks are properly purged from Thoas, with no chance of re-emerging, I want an orbital bombardment of the ruins. Flatten them. This is an unprofitable history for future settlers. This was not a culture here. It was an irrational mistake. Its memory has no place in my Father's Imperium.'

Iasus and Hierax saluted and left. Gage lingered.

'What is it?' Guilliman asked.

'We never saw anything that wasn't part of a military installation.'

'That's right.'

'Theoretical – if this fortress and its tunnels are what the culture of Thoas became, then this was a civilisation devoted entirely to war. That wouldn't be sustainable at all.'

'Not for any length of time on a single planet,' Guilliman agreed. 'And it clearly wasn't.' He took in Gage's troubled expression. 'There's something else, isn't there?' he asked.

'I was just thinking of the proportion of its resources the Imperium already devotes to war.'

'Which is precisely why the conclusion of the Great Crusade is necessary. You and I will be obsolete before very long, and I rejoice to think so.' He walked out of the chamber.

Gage stayed by the entrance, staring at the madness on the wall. 'How did they come to do this to themselves?' he wondered.

'Practical – the answers will simply be more squalor. This is not what humanity is, any more. We will confine this memory to the ashes with the orks.'

Gage consented to leave, then, but his expression was troubled as they headed to rejoin their forces, mustering at the entrance to what had become the ork crematorium.

Guilliman looked back once. He looked at the rows and hills of weapons. He looked at the ork throne, silhouetted in the light of guttering fires, and he wondered why, at this sight, he was overcome with a sense of blindness.

ABOUT THE AUTHOR

David Annandale is the author of the Horus Heresy novel *The Damnation of Pythos* and the Primarchs novel *Roboute Guilliman: Lord of Ultramar*. He has also written the Yarrick series, several stories involving the Grey Knights, and *The Last Wall*, *The Hunt for Vulkan* and *Watchers in Death* for The Beast Arises. For Space Marine Battles he has written *The Death of Antagonis* and *Overfiend*. He is a prolific writer of short fiction, including the novella *Mephiston: Lord of Death* and numerous short stories set in The Horus Heresy, Warhammer 40,000 and Age of Sigmar universes. David lectures at a Canadian university, on subjects ranging from English literature to horror films and video games.

An extract from

LEMAN RUSS
THE GREAT WOLF
by Chris Wraight

The hall rang with voices. Some were human, though those
voices were pale and thin beside the guttural roars of the tran-
shumans, the Ascended, the demigods. Braziers glowed with
coals, flaring up into blazes as the alcohol-rich *mjod* was flung
across them. The air was rich, a stink of sweat and cooked meats
and trodden straw.

This was deep in the Fang, enveloped within its iron-dark
innards, lit from within by writhing flame, a place of snaking
shadows and blood-red hearth-heat. The entire brotherhood was
there, brawling and gorging under the sight of their jarl, Aeska
Brokenlip, once warrior of Tra of the VI Legion, now Wolf Lord
of the Third Great Company of the Space Wolves Chapter. The
galaxy had changed since the breaking of the Siege, even in the
halls of Fenris, but much remained the same.

Aeska's Wolf Guard sat with him at the stone-hewn high table,
scrabbling across food boards for fat-rich intestines. They raised
gold-chased drinking horns, chucking oily liquid down hoarse

throats. They chanted the old songs of the Legion, the ones that had been sung on the ice world since before the Allfather had come, and which would be sung there after the last star was extinguished.

They wore armour, for this was a day of marking, of celebrating the raw strength of what had been dragged out of the galactic cataclysm and which now had borne fresh shoots, green like spear-thorns after the winter. They also wore furs, sticky with spillage, the trophies of the slain taken out in the wilderlands.

Haldor sat with his pack of Blooded Claws, the neophytes of the company, though on this day they had been given the place of honour below the high table. Eiryk was on his left, his face flushed, Valgarn on his right. It might have been any feast on any wood-built jarl's-hall in the midst of the high summer, with horns raised to honour the slain and goad the living.

Only after many hours did Brokenlip at last rise from his throne, shaking rust-brown hides from his shoulders, and the tide of noise shuddered into silence.

Aeska's face was scarred down the right-hand side, making the skin pale and puckered. One eye was augmetic, a ring of scratched metal bolted onto his skull; one hand was bionic. There were rumours that he had been taken from Yarant barely alive, his thread a second from being cut clean. He was one of the few, the ones who had stood beside Russ in the Age of Wonder, when all was new and the towers of the Imperium were first raised, and so when he spoke, even the Claws listened.

The Wolf Lord lifted a drinking-horn clutched in a gnarled, ring-studded fist.

'*Heilir, Fenryka,*' he growled, and his voice ran across the stone flags like wildfire kindling. 'Come in peace to this hearth.'

The greeting was as old as the bones of the world, and all raised their own drinks in response, saluting their warlord.

'We have come here under stone since Ogvai was jarl,' Aeska

said, 'to mark victory, to mark defeat, to blood the newcomers, to let our long-fangs beckon death a little closer.'

Coarse chuckles ran around the room.

'Yet this is the first night of a new age. These Claws who take their step into the Rout are the first to know nothing but new ways. All others here joined a Legion. They join a Chapter. They are our future.' Brokenlip switched his heavy gaze to Haldor's table, where it alighted on him above all. 'Allfather preserve us.'

Haldor held that gaze, not even acknowledging to himself how hard it was to meet the eyes of one who had fought for so long, so hard, against an enemy that even all these years after his final defeat still seemed as present as the dark on a fire's edge.

Brokenlip drew his blade – a great broadsword with a dragon's neck snaking along the serrated edge. He angled it towards the Claws, dipping it in salute.

'The enemy will return,' he said, his voice a low snarl that snagged like claws across hide. 'Fight it. Throttle it. Cast it down, just like we made you to do.'

The company clambered to their feet, shoving aside heavy wooden boards and reaching for chainswords, axes, longswords, mauls. All were held aloft, casting shadows of murder across the faces of the new recruits.

'When you came here, this was my hearth,' said Aeska, his pitted lips cracking into a fang-bared grimace, or perhaps a smile. 'Now it is yours. Defend it with your lives.'

They all cried aloud then, a fierce wall of sound that made the stone shiver and the flames shake.

'Vlka Fenryka!'

Before he knew what he was doing, Haldor had seized his axe. His pack had taken their own weapons, and they slid from battle-worn scabbards in a ripple of dry hisses.

'Fenrys!'

All of them were shouting now, summoning up spirits of war

and rage, fuelled by the punishing quantities of mjod coursing around their genhanced systems. The fires seemed to rear up, swelling within iron cages, pushing back the Mountain's eternal gloom.

Haldor was no different.

'Fenrys hjolda!'

The massed roars echoed back from the high chamber roof. Long Fang and Blooded Claw, Grey Hunter and Wolf Guard, the old names and the new, all became one voice amid the flames and the war-cries, bonded by the shared howl like the wolf packs of the outer wilds.

And then the thunder broke, replaced by the hard-edged, deep-timbre laughter of warriors. The weapons were stowed, the drinking-horns reached for. Brannak swaggered over to the Claws' table, his thick voice blurred by mjod, starting to tell the tales that would carry on far into the night. They would recite sagas now, all the grizzled warlords, reciting old records of old wars scattered far across the sea of stars. Every feast ended with this, the skjalds and the jarls remembering, for this was how annals were made on Fenris.

Throughout it all, Aeska kept his eyes fixed on Haldor. Once the last of the war-cries had faded, the Blooded Claw looked away from the high table, suddenly uncomfortable. He pushed his way from the bench, sending boards laden with raw meat thudding to the floor.

Eiryk looked back at him, his face mottled, eyes narrow with mirth. 'Too rich for you, brother?' he asked.

Haldor spat on the floor. He was fine. He was more than fine – he was bursting with life, his every muscle burning for the coming test of true combat.

Aeska's words echoed in his mind, though. *They are our future.*

'Listen to the old man's stories,' Haldor told him, holding up his empty drinking-horn. 'I thirst.'

He strode off, hearing Brannak's voice raised in declamation behind him.

'And the sky cracked, and the ice broke, and the Allfather came to Fenris, and Russ, war-girt, went to meet Him, and they fought, and the earth was lain waste, and the stars shivered out...'

Haldor shoved through the press of bodies, making his way towards the far gates of the hall. As he neared the great vats of heated mjod, as thick and viscous as unrefined promethium, a chill wind sighed through the open arches. Beyond those arches, empty corridors snaked away into the heart of the Mountain, unlit and cold, burrowing ever deeper. He looked at them, and they looked back at him.

Haldor turned on the threshold and saw his battle-brothers celebrating. Thralls scuttled across the floor, veering around the giants with silent skill, carrying more fuel for the revels.

This was his world now, his hearth to guard.

He slipped out under the nearest arch. The air temperature soon dropped away to the hellish default, and the last of the firelight flickered into nothing.

Haldor pressed himself against frigid stone, rough-cut and slick with ice. He took in a deep breath, enjoying the searing cold in his lungs. The dark pressed around him, just as it had in the forests of Asaheim, blue-black, vengeful.

Then he was moving again, loping like he had done before, deeper down. He did not know all the ways of the Mountain yet. Perhaps no Sky Warrior did, for the fortress was never more than a fraction full. The great bulk of the Chapter was forever at war, coming back to the home world only for feasts or councils, and in any case the place had been intended for a Legion.

He went on, further away, deeper down. The echoes of mortal voices died away entirely, replaced by the almost imperceptible rhythm of the deep earth. Ice cracked endlessly, ticking like a chrono in the dark. Meltwater, formed over buried power lines, trickled across broken stone before freezing again in swirling patterns below. From the great shafts came the half-audible growls of the massive reactors tended by the Iron Priests, and the eternal forges that created the Chapter's weapons of war, and, so he had heard tell, the forgotten halls where the eldest of all dwelt, their hearts locked in ice and their minds kept in a stasis of dreams.

By then he had no idea where he was going, nor why, only that the shadows were welcome, and for the moment he had no need of fire to warm his hearts nor more flesh to fill his innards. He had been changed, and his body embraced the crippling cold where once it would have killed him, and he welcomed it.

Then he froze, and the hairs on the back of his arms lifted. Soundlessly, swift as a thought, he reached for the haft of the axe bound at his belt.

The corridor ahead was as dark and empty as all the others, rising slightly and curving to the left. Haldor narrowed his gaze, but the shadow lay heavy, and nothing broke the gloom.

Something was there, up ahead, out of visual range but detectable all the same. A pheromone, perhaps, or the ghost of a scent. Haldor dropped low and crept forwards, keeping the haft gripped loose. The tunnels of the Fang were full of dangers, all knew that. He became painfully aware of how noisy his armour was, and how much stealthier he could be without it.

He reached the curve ahead and passed around it. The change in the air told him the corridor had opened out, but the dark was now unbroken. He could hear something out there – breathing, like an animal's, soft and low – but could not pin it down. He crouched, shifting the weight of the axe, readying to move.

Before he could do anything more, a voice came out of the darkness, deeper than any animal's, rimed with age.

'Put the axe down, lad.'

Haldor had obeyed before he even knew it, bound by a

gene-heritage that was older than he was. Suddenly, the pall seemed to shift, and a figure loomed up through the Fang's under-murk. For a moment, all Haldor saw was a figment of old race-nightmares – a daemon of the darkling woods, crowned with branches, eyes as blue as sea-ice and hands like the gnarled roots of trees.

But then he was looking into features he knew as well as his own, despite never having seen them in flesh and blood. The face was smeared with ashes, a daub-pattern of black on pale skin. A heavy mantle of furs hung over hunched shoulders, and a gunmetal-grey gauntlet clutched at the hilt of a heavy, rune-encrusted longsword.

Instantly, without being bidden, Haldor dropped to one knee.

'Enough of that,' said his primarch, testily. 'Why are you here?'

Haldor didn't know. Aeska's words had driven him out, and the cold had sucked him in, but that was all he understood. Perhaps it had been the drink, or perhaps the last chance to walk the silent depths before war called, or maybe the tug of fate.

Now he stood, alone, in the presence of the Lord of Winter and War.

'One of Aeska's whelps,' said Leman Russ, drawing closer, his strange eyes shining in the dark. 'No wonder you left the hall. Bloody sagas. I've heard them all.'

Haldor couldn't tell if he was jesting. 'They told of the All-father,' he said, hesitantly, wary of the danger in the primarch's every move. Russ was like a blackmane, huge, unpredictable, bleeding with danger. 'They said you fought Him. The only time you lost.'

Russ barked out a laugh, and the fur mantle shook. 'Not the only time.' He shrank back into the shadows then, seeming to diminish a fraction, but the danger remained.

Haldor caught snatched glimpses of his master's garb. Not the heavy armour plate of the warrior-king, but layers of hard-spun wool, streaked with the charcoal of spent embers. They were the clothes of death rites, of mourning. Some warrior of the Aett, perhaps even the *Einherjar*, must have been slain, though it was unusual for the Wolf Priests not to have called out the names of the dead through the Chapter.

Russ noticed the weapon Haldor had placed back at his belt, and looked at it strangely. 'You know what blade that is?' he asked.

Haldor shook his head, and Russ snorted in disgust.

'The gaps grow, holes in the ice, greater with every summer-melt,' the primarch said. 'You know nothing. They remember nothing.'

Russ trailed off, half turning back towards the dark. Haldor said nothing. His hearts were both beating, a low thud, an instinctive threat-response even when no blades were raised.

'I know not whether you were sent to mock me or bring me comfort,' Russ said at last, 'but sent you were. So listen. Listen and remember.'

Haldor stayed where he was, not daring to move, watching the huge, fur-clad outline under the Mountain's heart. Russ was speaking like a skjald.

'I fought the Allfather, that is true, and He bested me, for the gods themselves fear Him, mightiest of men. But that was not the only time.'

The eyes shone, points of sapphire, lost in the grip of ice-shadow.

'There was another.'